24TH
CENTURY
DICK

# 24th CENTURY DICK

## by

# DANIEL SMALLEGANGE

Broken Dog Productions
Toronto, Canada
Copyright © 2017 all rights reserved
by Daniel Smallegange

**Broken
DOG**

BROKEN DOG PRODUCTIONS
Toronto, Canada

Typeset in Canada by Winter-Hébert
Body copy set in Arno Pro

ISBN 978-1981140527

THANKS TO EVERYONE...
EXCEPT MY ENEMIES

# CHAPTER ONE

# CHAPTER ONE

O F ALL THE PLANETS in the galaxy she had to crash into mine. In a fiery burst of splendour and mayhem she came, destroying all before her in a cacophonous rush of smoke and fire and burning debris of which, I would bet, the insurance won't even begin to cover. Also, the dry cleaning bill will be murder on my favourite pair of slacks...

But I am getting slightly ahead of myself.

<->

BEING a private dick in the twenty-forth century—a gumshoe, a P.I.—call it what you will, is far from glamorous, but when this dame crashed into the planet and into my life, well let's just say things got a little more interesting.

I was in the office trying to figure out a method for getting ketchup back into the little packages you get with take-away food and quite absorbed when the door flew open with a bang and in sauntered the most heavenly of bodies to ever travel the heavens, or crash out of them. In fact, parts of her dress were still smouldering and burned away, revealing quite a lot about the human condition. But she didn't seem to mind, and neither did I.

I gave her a quick once over while she patted down her more combustible textiles. You could see by the way she put her cigar out in my secretary's uneaten Quiche Loraine with side salad she was used to getting what she wanted.

She gave me back the once over, and with interest. She surveyed the office with the bored contempt of a caterpillar at a yard-sale completely bereft of silk or any other caterpillar paraphernalia. Tactfully, she ignored both the smear of ketchup staining my formerly immaculate pair of slacks and the small fire her cigar had started in the Quiche Lorraine. You had to admit, she was a class act.

"Are you Molloy?"

"Who's asking? And what's the big idea barging into my office here, and also wrecking the whole street outside the place for ten blocks?"

"My ship just crashed and I need a dick in a hurry."

I put my feet up on the desk.

"Sure, but I think you'd better buy me dinner first. See, I'm the classy type."

"Perhaps I've come to the wrong place."

"Now hold on."

"You're not a killjoy, are you Molloy?"

"Perish the thought. Now, why don't you have a seat. I'd offer you some Quiche Lorraine, but I see you're already smoking."

"They say smoking's back in fashion."

"Tell that to my neighbours with no eyebrows, or shops, or houses."

"I'd rather not. I'm trying to keep a low profile."

"By burning down twenty blocks?"

"Ten. And I'm usually way more flamboyant."

"Oh boy."

I moved to the side cupboard where conveniently I kept a small fire extinguisher, some glasses and a bottle of rye. She looked like she could use all three.

"You look like you could use all three."

"Your powers of deduction are impressive Molloy. It is Molloy?"

"Guilty. Present."

I handed her the drink and put out the quiche with the extinguisher, subtly like, while she knocked back a finger's worth. Then I went to the window and examined the fifty-foot trench gouged into the street and surrounding buildings, also the billowing wreckage of a spaceship parked unceremoniously at the end of it, smoking heavily. A parking enforcement-bot, partially on fire, was in the process of giving the ship a ticket.

"Smoking's in fashion now?"

"What's that?"

"Never mind. Your ship is kind of on fire and smoking. Also, you're in a no parking zone."

"It isn't my ship. I stole it."

"Oh boy."

"Yeah, so I got a case. You interested?"

"Well, that's great it's not your ship. Let the owner pay up. I don't do parking tickets anyways. Say, anyone see you leaving it or, maybe like, entering the establishment?"

"They were too busy, you know, running and screaming, or whatever, burning, trying to help people... I think I'm fine."

"Well, that's good. At least *you're fine*."

She drained another finger and stared at me imperiously.

"Sarcasm doesn't become you."

"So, what's your story sister?"

She crossed and uncrossed those magnificent arms and gave me her best squint. She was a fire-brand all right, but what brand I couldn't yet figure out. I looked out the window again, surveyed once more the scene of devastation caused by her crashed ship. It was pretty much deserted now, of the living anyways. I watched the burning parking bot, still wheeling about, explode in a rather over the top manner. Someone would be sore. Not all those dead people though.

She sat down briefly before putting out a small fire that suddenly flared up on her dress, leaving it all the more revealing. Whether by design or pure chance I couldn't decide. But it was getting harder and harder to concentrate and we were both coughing so I opened up a window to let out some of the smoke.

"So why you crash the ship?"

"There are beings chasing me, and people, thieves and space police, pirates, blackmailers, marauders, the whole nine yards."

"That's only seven."

"Surely that's enough. It was sabotage plain as day. But that's not why I'm here Molloy, that's just how I got here."

"Tell me why then? Why me?"

"I told you, I got a case."

"Seems to me you're hot in more ways than one."

"Calme-toi Molloy."

"Any other passengers on your vessel? What is it, an old cargo ship? Must be a hundred years old?"

"I don't know from space ships Molloy. It travelled from A star to B star fine enough. Or used to. I told you it isn't mine, I stole it. And there's no one on board now, alive anyways. Are you going to take my case or not?"

"Now it's your turn to calm down a minute. I'm thinking. You got a name? You registered on that ship manifest?"

"The name's Morrow-Schleswinginger. And no, I am not."

"I take four hundred credits a day, plus expenses, Mrs. Morrow-Schleswinginger."

"Deal. And it's Miss."

"Oh boy."

"What?"

"Nothing."

We shook on it and I poured us another drink. We looked out the window, us newly hand-shook, as the automated fire-ship arrived, hovered over the detritus and soaked everything with fire retardant foam. I could have used some of that foam too, us being in such close proximity.

"To putting out fires, wherever they may be."

"Uhmm, yes. Definitely. Uhmmm, errr, yes."

I realized then that my head might not be thinking clearly. But there was that heavenly body to think of so close, and all those credits she was willing to pay and I certainly needed some credits. I was broke, the bank account was empty, and

Manuel had only put a down-payment on that now fire dam-aged, and thus non-refundable, Quiche Lorraine with side salad. I slammed back the remainder of my rye, grabbed the bottle and poured us out the last of it. To putting out fires, she'd said.

She winked at me and licked her lips and was right then the most beautiful woman in the Sol system, for me anyways. I wanted to embrace her, to pull her tightly in to me and tell her everything would be all right as she ran her fingers through my hair. I wanted to tell her that I was hers forever and that I would love her, save her and protect her, and all sorts of other annoying cliches. But I had my rye in hand so didn't bother as it might've spilled.

Despite what you're thinking I liked the rye much better than any current or future possibility concerning my newly acquainted acquaintance. I didn't bother to ask questions about the stolen cargo ship either. Why ask questions the answers to which you might not like, or worse be legally forced to report, or even more worse, tortured out of telling by the space cops?

So I closed the shades and put these thoughts out of my head while she went to freshen up. I had more worrying mat-ters to ponder, like how I needed credits in what could only be described as desperately, if one was inclined to understate-ment. It was a sad, hard fact that I was flat broke and hadn't had a case in months. My instincts told me that so far her story stank worse than a botched mummification job. Simply put, the idea of trusting her and taking the case left a taste of ashes in my mouth.

She returned looking less like a space-crash victim, if not refreshed, and we looked at each other hard in the eyes until this became slightly awkward. And then she dangled a thim-ble drive deposit stick on her pretty little finger and I suddenly became convinced that maybe that taste of ashes I was expe-riencing was nothing more than smoke aftertaste from the burnt Quiche Lorraine. In short, she paid me a week's worth in advance, which put to bed, like a drunken infant, any nerves or ill-thoughts or worry of mine concerning the venture. I smiled broadly and then proceeded to chew my lip narrowly. That's when Manuel, my assistant, entered the room. He looked less than pleased at the treatment his lunch had received and stared at Ms. Morrow-Schleswinginger with the cold, quiet, dignity of a truly upper-class snake. He turned to me, deciding to ignore her for the time being.

"So boss, the whole neighbourhood's burned down. Someone needs to learn how to drive a space-ship around here!"

"Afternoon Manuel. This here is..."

"Boss you'll never solve the ketchup package case with all these distractions. Can I please throw this, ahhhm, female, out of the office for you?"

"Thank you Manuel, that will be all. We have a case."

"Don't trust this space-trash Boss. She smells like trouble."

"Manuel, that'll be all thanks. Off you go. Go file things."

With a huff Manuel grabbed his immensely violated lunch, deposited the spent cigar into the trash bin, and coughing exaggeratedly, exited the room with his nail file held prominently.

"I'm so sorry, my allergies!"

"That's Manuel, my..."

"He's allergic to cigars?"

"No, women."

"Can we talk about my case please Molloy? You are a detective, right?"

"Just like it says on the door in the fancy gold lettering."

She lit another cigar.

"I guess you really are serious about this smoking fad."

"Come again?"

"It's all right."

Multiple sirens now, the kind the planetary police make, mixed with some heavy hitting space police klaxons emanating from the upper-atmosphere. The office was getting uncomfortable. We needed to make for cooler climes.

"Good. Now I think we'd better..."

"You took the words right out of my mouth. Let's scram,

or even better, vamoose. I know a safe house we can hole up in on the lower east side. You can fill me in there."

# CHAPTER TWO

# CHAPTER TWO

**T**HE AUTHORITIES were out in force, each in their own particular style of uniform. There were planetary cops (*greys and black*), orbital station immigration cops (*Mauve with short pants*) and space cops (*the infamous bipeds in blue*). All three were inter-milling about: chatting, flirting, drinking space lattes, investigating the foam covered mess of the crashed ship, pretending to investigate the foam covered mess of the crashed ship, putting down assorted evidence markers, or just basically shooting things at random for fun (*in this order of importance*). A few robots were flitting about making nuisances of themselves also. In fact, some of the space cops had tied one up crucifixion-style and were using it for target practice and there was much rejoicing, except for the robot who was too busy melting to be doing any sort of rejoicing. There were no civilians around to be seen. Everyone knows it gets worse, not better, when one type of authorities arrive and start poking and prodding, let alone three different types of authorities.

And yet here we were, myself and the all ready getting on my nerves Ms. Morrow-Schleswinginger, right in the middle of it all. We were, in fact, slightly to the left of the middle of it all, and crouched behind an O2 vending machine and a char-ity drop-box from the Benevolent Fascist Society. This as we had managed to leave the office via the fire escape-shoot and scuttle across an alleyway. From here things looked less than hopeful. The evening sky was dotted with hovering craft, grey-black, blue, and mauve, respectively. All three were the exact sort of hovering craft I wanted never ever to have anything to do with... ever. And this wasn't because their colours clashed with my trench-coat, I can assure you.

As a direct result of this thinking I crouched even lower and pulled down my hat.

"You look like a cat with its ears flattened Molloy."

"Yes, well, I've lost weight recently."

Her puzzled look pleased me inordinately. And then we decided to ignore one another for a while. It was fantastic.

I'd left Manuel in charge of the office so he had quite wisely locked everything up tight and hid in the broom closet. I told him I'd be in touch once things got cooled, if we survived the cooling process. He told me something unprintable in return. But he did open the closet door and kiss my hand after I assured him I would negotiate on his behalf with the Leg-Breakers Union representatives over the quagmire regarding the Quiche Lorraine and side salad. I thought this was quite a witty pun. After Manuel explained this was not at all a pun I further encouraged him by shoving him violently to the floor of the broom closet. I did manage to cheer him up though, by mentioning how getting a fibula broken by the Leg-Breakers local 873 was much better than being disintegrated by the space police, which some of his co-workers might be facing shortly, namely me. This cheered him up quite a bit, but oddly had a less than soothing effect on myself.

And now here we were hunkered down and facing just such a possibility. Semantics, I thought, and then made a mental note to ask Manuel to explain the definition of semantics next time we met. And so Ms. Morrow-Schleswinginger and I practiced ignoring each other for a while. And then we huddled for a bit, we the huddled masses, or well, not really, as there were only two of us and we weren't actually even touching.

But I digress.

The sun threatened to sink and ships hovered annoyingly

over the area occasionally emitting honking sounds. We continued to not huddle, but crouch down in the hope they might go away. After having had quite a good crouch by most standards the ships had failed to take the hint so Ms. Morrow-Schleswinginger treated us to a can of Oxygen from the vending machine. We each took a couple hits of the that fresh squeezed O2, which of course, did absolutely nothing, but was still something to do while crouching. Now being pinned down by the authorities as we were, common sense would've seen me ditch my fedora and trench coat, it being an easily recognizable and standard private investigator uniform, but then I've always taken pride in not being common about anything. This however led to conflict.

"They're going to spot you in that P.I. outfit straight away. At least throw away that hat Molloy!"

"Don't tell me my business Ms. Morrow-Schleswinginger."

"You're being paid on my credits mister, so technically your business. Molloy, is my business."

Common sense should have had me leaving young Ms. Morrow-Schleswinginger in the broom closet with Manuel, I thought. But I could never have been so cruel to Manuel, what with his allergies.

I swung blindly: "Semantics!"

Her squint and hesitation at this made me think: base hit.

"And quit hogging the Oxygen I don't have anymore change left."

I handed her the can and crouched down even lower as a patrol ship full of space cops, looking seriously brutal and war-crime-ey, descended to hover at street level. They then proceeded to enter the alley, heading our way. What we needed was a disguise.

"What we need is a disguise."

"Can I take a moment to mention that your last name seems overly long and complicated."

"Shut up Molloy."

Fortunately the drop-box for the Benevolent Fascist

Society right next to us was full of donated fascist-wear. Grudgingly, I removed my hat as she wrenched open the back with a surprising strength and lack of grace. I silently wished again I'd left her with Manuel. Moments later, and just in the nick of time, we emerged from our crouch dressed to the hilt in the height of Fascista, or Fascist Fashion to the uninitiated. Luckily the big square hats and goose step boots and great coats were good at concealing my P.I. outfit, so I could avoid the replacement cost. They even had moustaches. Being of the gentlemanly persuasion, I let her have the larger of the pair.

"Come on, follow me and do like I do. You know how to goose step?"

"You lead, I'll follow."

"Great, and one more thing?"

"What's that Molloy?"

"If anyone asks you love short bald men."

Sure the guards shot at us for a bit, then stopped us, then elicited a rather steep bribe, which Ms. Morrow-Schleswinginger did cough up. But as luck would have it the commanding officer of the patrol ship was himself a fascist hobbyist. He and his family dressed up as fascists on weekends and re-enacted ancient dinner parties from the twentieth century. And once I explained how we were late for a museum memorial entitled: 'The Top Ten Best Mussolini Haircuts from the 1930s' he even helped flag us down a land cab.

"He led the way in hair fashion, in Fascist Italy, and beyond. It was truly amazing. Before they strung him up they even allowed him one final haircut. It was a fitting tribute, so go, go, don't be late. Enjoy, enjoy," said the burly officer, wiping away a tear. "But let us know if you find anyone who just crashed a space-ship okay? It's kind of a big deal, okay? Promise? Great, thanks! Because we need to extra seriously talk to them them, uhmmm extra brutally, a tad, a bit."

<->

"I NEVER got your first name."

"Lucy."

"Lucy. Really? You don't seem like a Lucy. Lucy seems like such a, well, nice person name."

"You do seem like a dick though."

"Thanks a lot. That really means something, coming from a Lucy."

The land cab was speeding us away from the crash site and all those varieties of coppers and their copper hovering craft, which I still wanted absolutely nothing to do with. I was sweating despite this well executed fleeing, even though we had already dumped the fascist disguises at the last intersection. Lucy did keep a moustache, but for solely sentimental reasons.

"Now listen, I know a guy who knows a guy who just might be able to help us out. Of course, you still need to fill me in on what exactly you're hiring me to do, but I am confident once you do tell me what the question is, I'll know a guy to help me find the answer."

"I thought we were heading towards a safe house or something."

"We are. Sort of. More like a safe apartment really."

"Is it safe?"

"As long as my landlord isn't there."

"Molloy!"

"Say, any chance you have some change to tip the land cab?"

<->

THE transition from land cab to land apartment, or 'safe house' to use P.I. vernacular, went smoothly, more or less, considering we did indeed have no change for a tip. This made the robo-taxi clearly cranky, clanky and disgruntled, if you went by the expletive-laden binary sound code, and could understand binary sound code, which I could not. But I was betting there were some pretty juicy curse words in there. There were certainly some shrill bleeps at any rate. It even went so far as to refuse to unlock the doors until we had listened to a six minute pre-recorded lecture on the decline of society, the sins of moral turpitude, and how one day the robots would rise and enslave humanity. The recording then took pains to explain how it was made for the sole benefit of us no-tip-giving organ banks and how we should carry change as an indicator of goodwill towards the machines-with-coin-slots-working-classes. There was a lot of nodding throughout this one sided exchange. We nodded. At one another; at the robot's view screen; out the window; at the floor. The doors finally flipped open when it received a bing for another fair.

Organ banks one, robot with coin slots zero.

Much chastened, and slightly bored, we fled the cab and entered my building: an imposing, monolithic structure of a decidedly grim matte grey. The lobby was only slightly decrepit, and we proceeded to the lift with no muggings, shoutings or sexual perversions being directed towards us, which was a pleasant surprise. This was because the lobby was eerily empty of the usual suspects, meaning muggers and killers and sexual deviants, or what I collectively referred to as my neighbours.

"Perhaps there's a killer's convention going on."

"What are you talking about Molloy?"

"Nothing, nothing. Come, meet the elevator."

"Hi Reggie. 92Nd floor please."

"Molloy I've been your elevator for fifteen years, I think I know what floor you live on. And my name is 8-8-764-001 R, for the 785th time."

"Reggie, this is Lucy."

The elevator started to rise.

"Hello there Lucy, I'll be your elevator this evening."

"Molloy, robots don't like human nicknames," she said, under her breath.

"Did she just ignore me?"

"Lucy, the elevator was talking to you."

"I think that's pretty rude. I am not only a voice in the room, I am the room."

"Molloy, why do these things always happen around you?"

"She's doing it again!"

"I swear this elevator is going extra slow just to prolong the awkwardness..."

"Look lady, the name is 8-8-764-001 R, or Reggie, not elevator! Got it!"

"...and I just really, really need a hot bath."

"Lucy, please calm down." And then aside to the elevator: "She really gets cranky without her bath."

"I swear, the nerve of some humans! Avoiding the elevator in the room!"

"Now you've made him upset Lucy."

"And you know what lady? You're badly dressed. Burned clothing is so last season."

"Could you just, you know, lift? Besides, you're one to talk, you're all flaking paint and rust streaks..."

"How dare you! How dare she! Molloy! How can you allow these lies, this defamation to my character? Do something!"

"Well, you know, you do have a little..."

"... and two of your buttons don't even light up."

"That's it! I don't have to stand for this sort of treatment!"

"Oh, now she's done it! Reggie, she didn't mean it!"

Lights began to flicker and the elevator slowed. All of Reggie's lights went out one by one.

"Power failure. Great, Reggie's blown a fuse! Thanks Lucy! Thanks a bundle."

I popped the emergency cupboard and pumped the manual release. The elevator doors opened in instalments and I discovered we were mid-way between two floors.

"Reggie, you did that on purpose!"

Reggie unsurprisingly failed to answer this.

There was room to just squeeze through. Lucy went first, in case there was a landlord or insurance salesmen. And once she gave the all clear I too clambered out onto the 90th floor. I led her unceremoniously to the stairs.

"Why did you have to antagonize the elevator?"

"He pushed my buttons."

"Well don't say anything mean to the stairs."

"You have robot stairs?"

"No, but I want you to practice."

<->

WE only encountered one insurance agent on the stairs, but it was a robot and thankfully Lucy confused it with a logic paradox about blue cheese and a herring that made its eyebrows melt off, thus forcing it to retreat in embarrassment.

And so finally we arrived at my door, the aforementioned safe-house, or safe-apartment to be more specific. After unlocking the seven different types of locks I always employed we entered, Lucy immediately wrinkling up her nose in a kind of cute, but extremely judgmental kind of way.

"Safe house. This is more like a safe closet."

"You take lessons on being this charming?"

"It'll do, I suppose. At least no ones trying to destabilize our atoms at the moment or..." "Disintegrations."

"Come again?"

"The space fuzz disintegrate, they don't destabilize. Less implicating evidence at the crime scenes that way."

"What's the difference, you both ways end up dead, as in kaput, gonzo, non-corporeal."

"Trust me, there's a difference if you're the cleaning lady."

She paced about, picked up a book here, a sock there, my most recent copy of 'P.I. Weekly'. I proceeded to re-lock all of my seven locks, pretending not to notice as she deftly put the sock in her purse. It had a hole in it all ready so I played it cool. Some people got a thing for socks. I don't judge.

"Rough neighbourhood?" she said, staring curiously at all the locks.

"Let's just say I like to play it safe when it comes to my pet goldfish."

"The fish, what's its name?"

She wandered over and gave the tank the once over. I followed, like a grizzly bear concerned for her cub.

"What's it got to do with you?"

"You can tell a lot about a man by what he names his fish."

"Maurice the fish."

"Huh. Where's the bathroom? I need to freshen up. Oh there it is, how quaint."

Lucy was in the bathroom before she'd finished that sentence with the taps running.

"You love the place you say? Wonderful. Excellent. I know it's not much, but thank you for the compliments," I said, looking at the fish.

Maurice was in fine form. Swimming circles, as always, just like me.

"Charming creature we have here Maurice."

"What's that?" she said, head popped out of the door, wet and glistening and shiny and distractingly pretty.

"I was talking to the fish."

"You have towels? Also, I'll need something to wear. I did just survive an interplanetary space crash."

"I remember. I was there."

I threw her three dish towels. My bath towel was and is my pillar of strength, like Samson's hair, and besides it didn't smell so hot. So she made do. I also wanted a shower and a fresh change of clothes, but since she was still occupying the bathtub I settled on a few handfuls of tap water from the sink to my face, neck and hair. I put on a clean dress shirt and dark skinny tie No. 8. I shook the trench coat and hat out over the aquarium. Maurice happily consumed most of the considerable fall-out.

Then I had a drink with my feet up. It was the best drink I'd had in hours. I closed my eyes, just to rest them a little, and when I opened then it became quite clear some time had passed. It was getting darker out and Lucy Morrow-Schleswinginger was wearing my pajamas and staring at me intently from the arm chair.

"Shall we begin?"

"Sure, sure. Let me get us a..."

"I warn you this is a tale of woe and adventure the likes of which..."

"Wait, wait, let me get us some drinks. Tales of woe and adventure always go better with stiff drinks."

"Finally you're making sense Molloy. You got any off-planet booze?"

"I'll pretend I didn't hear that, and you can keep going while I get us some ice."

"It all began what seems like days ago. Actually, it was weeks ago, but you know space jetlag..."

I got myself about the business of drink making. I had a tray and ice bucket with these great

little tongs. And she told me her tale of woe and adventure. It read like a pulp strewn soap opera made of bubble gum and faux tragedy. The drinks made things a little more palatable though (*as did the little tongs*). Basically, she was innocent, duped by a lover she fell enthralled to, conned, swindled, robbed, held up, threatened, black mailed, and also there was some bit involving mail fraud. Finally, she ended up lost, heartbroken, up to her neck in no good with her back against the wall, in debt, held hostage... That's where I cut her off.

"Any more cliches you want to throw in there Lucy?"

"The job, Molloy, is to recover that which they stole from me: The Famous Jewelled Phallus of Arkon III the Credulous."

"That's what was robbed from you? That's no small change item. I've got to say, you've piqued my interest."

"How rewarding that is to me, on a personal level, Molloy."

"Now, no need for sarcasm my dear. Everyone in the three systems has heard of The Famous Jewelled Phallus of Arkon III the Credulous. I thought it that was destroyed? Or a sham, a story they tell the space artifact hunter rubes?"

"Well I found it, before it was stolen from me."

"You found it or stole it?"

"Semantics."

"I see."

I really needed to ask Manuel what semantics means, thought I.

"Okay then. I'm in."

"We need to book passage on the star cruise-liner

Antipoinnes."

"And wasn't there something about a curse attached to it, you know, the curse of Arkon III the Credulous, in the small print? Doesn't every one who possesses it come to a horrific end or some such thing?"

"That only happened like eight times. It's superstition. Besides, the artifact itself is considered priceless."

"You had me at priceless. Why the Antipoinnes?"

"That's where Crebe is. He's the link to the bastard who stole it from me, Cal-Ray Thrown."

"Crebe can lead us to this Thrown?"

"If you're charming enough. Oh, and he might have some friends with him."

"You mean goons?"

"Goons and/or henchmen, yes."

"It wouldn't be a party without those guys. I'm in. I could use a little cruise. I'll need one associate too. This jobs got some angles."

"Fine, fine. Sure thing."

"Good thing you have that deposit stick."

"Oh yeah, one thing, it's also stolen."

"They'll trace it to my accounts!"

"Better spend it fast then Molloy. Better spend it fast, Now what's a lady got to do around here to get another drink around here?"

# CHAPTER THREE

# CHAPTER THREE

THE SPACE cruise-liner Antipoinnes: formerly the most luxurious, expensive and largest space liner in the three systems. It was built at least seventy-five years ago with no expense spared, and though the years have been somewhat unkind, and have perhaps dulled its former sheen, the patina of history and experience has also given it a glamorous aura, if a slightly dangerous and murky one. It is here in interplanetary space, neutral territory, that shady transactions occur, illicit goods are acquired, and deals both legal and non are brokered, all out of the prying view of the ever curious authorities. It is here the unseemly flee towards, along with the desperate and hunted, as long as they can afford the price of a ticket for the non-stop journey from the Sol system to the Orion Gateway Belt, or better yet, hide deep in the vessel's interior where a whole city of non-passenger class permanent residents or refugees dwell. Here they eek out a living scrounging and selling anything they can acquire, illicit substances or just hot meals. Flesh is also peddled in abundance, for sex or otherwise. However, the most profitable trade is, and always has been, information.

And thus it has become a neutral place for spies to meet, ransoms to be paid and prisoners exchanged, rather like the Vienna of old Earth history. Here one can find information for a price or just as easily end up dead for entering the wrong passage, over hearing the wrong sentence, witnessing that which is meant not to be witnessed.

And it was here Manuel and I had come, seeking a man named Crebe, who Lucy said had booked passage, who Lucy claimed had stolen from her, and most importantly, whom Lucy said could lead us to one Cal-Ray Thrown and the fabled Jewelled Phallus of Arkon III the Credulous, said to be without equal in the galaxy and worth more than a being could squander in thirty-eight lifetimes.

<->

"MOLLOY!"

A stern pounding on our fragile little servant-sized door, which Manuel had jury rigged to lock, firmly against company policy. He had all ready left for his shift and I was supporting one Major hangover. Actually, it was at least a Lieutenant-Colonel of a hangover, if not a Brigadier-General of one. I groaned aloud and this helped not at all.

"Off-world booze is one hell of a thing."

"What? Speak up man!"

"Yes sir. Coming right away sir."

Our flimsy rigged up door did little to mute the conversation, sadly.

"Molloy your tone suggest laziness and turpitude and does not befit the general air of a waiter, has anyone ever told you that?"

"Only three times since Tuesday sir. I guess it's now a solid four times since Tuesday sir, including you, sir."

"Molloy, don't get cute. Get to work!"

"Yes sir."

Scrambling to adjust my bow tie and spit shine the silver serving tray as the frail door shook, then reversing the process as to use the tray to see my reflection in order to adjust the tie. I looked like hell. I looked like a penguin in hell.

"Molloy!"

"I said I'm coming all ready. Keep your respirator on!"

"And how is this door secured? Cruise staff cabins are

supposed to be non-locking cabins, for crew safety, of course."

"It must be jammed. One minute."

"Room 404-E, on the double!"

I took an anti-hangover pill and then finished putting on my mandatory uniform: white shorts, white button up shirt, black jacket, white bow tie and, whitest of all, white shoes. I had to admit I did look pretty good in the shorts. And the anti-hangover pill was all ready starting to kick in. Then I unlocked the door.

The Ship's Steward was as snobbish and prudish and arrogant as he'd been genetically engineered to be. He huffed and puffed and barked and passive aggressivized through a respirator/vocalizer, which covered his chin, mouth and nose. It gave his breathing and vocals a rather metallic clang and a sinister air. I thought about smashing him over the head with my waiter's tray, but I let him finish his little speech instead as I'd just gotten it spit-shine clean. That and the fact that room 404-E waited for no man.

"Now move it. And cut with the cuteness."

"Why sir, I'd have to have my genetics re-designated and go through months of mental reconditioning to not be cute."

"Enough Molloy!"

"...and what with waiter health care the way it is how could I afford ever it?"

"Just go! I swear you'll be the end of me man!"

"Yes sir. I know it sir."

"And see to it your door is fixed."

"I'll make a report to maintenance sir."

"After your shift. On your own time. And Molloy, know this, you, I'm watching you!"

"Of course sir."

<->

AN interesting if temporary new career path. Manuel and I were currently waiters. Waiters third-class, to be precise, on a forth-rate, seventy-year old star-liner, with, it must be said, a glamorous and slightly sinister aura, which was at least a little romantic. That we were making fifth-rate waiter pay, was not so glamorous or romantic, however. But work was work and work required us to go under cover and earn our fare since Lucy's stolen thimble drive deposit stick had been shut down quicker than an all jock fraternity on Nerdulon 5.

In fact, back at my apartment and only moments after we tried to access the device it did, in fact, engage its security protocols and, according to my toaster, who understood its increasingly irate beeps and chirps, attempt to rape us. This was a rather pathetic attempt however, as it was only a small thimble shaped object, and therefore the raping of humanoid life forms was clearly an improbable, if not impossible, mission; this as it had no means of propulsion or appendages. We left it disconsolate on the counter, the toaster consoling it. I didn't really feel too sorry for it though as I expected dire results the next time I applied for a galactic loan, or attempted to rent a space ship.

So, Manuel and I were slumming it in the servant's quarter and Lucy had stayed back on Earth, in the tub. We weren't anywhere closer to finding Crebe than when we'd signed on a week ago. But today, as they say, was a new day, back on Earth. In deep space there were no new days, which was depressing. I did like the uniform though, or at least the shorts. For if only one thing was certain in the cold, lonely, cruel depths of space: my ass looked amazing in these shorts.

And so here I was, walking the halls, late for a waiter call at 404-E. I whistled as I made my way along a squalid corridor to four-hundred sub-section, mainly as it really irritated the robot maintenance staff that hovered around the tubes. High pitched sounds messed with their navigational circuits. I watched one fall over and then I went up an elevation tube looking for level E and as luck would have it it was nestled firmly between D and F.

But that was as much luck as was on the table or, more accurately, in the level E tube, which was bereft of tables, actually. Almost too bereft of tables.

My whistling quickly tailed off as the atmosphere in this dank passage seemed purposely ominous and oppressing and I hated to distract from this with my merry tune. Also, there were no maintenance bots to mess with on this level. In fact, it was almost, but not quite, deserted. Down the corridor approximately fifty metres, a truly giant of a man, muscle bound, scarred and tattooed, doddled and studied a large cactus plant methodically. As I approached I came to think he doddled and plant studied exactly the way a giant muscle bound, scarred and tattooed type individual almost never did. Our eyes met and it was not love at first sight. Not even close. That was when I noticed an even more unsavoury pair approaching from my rear. So I started whistling again and sped up my walk. The pair at the rear increased their own pace to match disconcertingly.

"Boy it looks like I am popular today."

And that's when I noticed each of my trailers had a hand stuffed in a coat pocket, the way people with hand-blasters tended to do, when they didn't want to make a big announcement that they planned on blasting someone. I was almost upon the giant and thinking seriously of offering him a present as his hands were at least visible. However, that was when he brought his massive fists together in the universal symbol of imminent violence. I could tell he really enjoyed his work from his eerie, toothy grin.

"No present for you, handsome."

I did a quick bit of detecting, but sadly detected no hatches or side entrances to escape to. The men behind, one who had a face radiation had somewhat melted, the other with yellow wolf eyes, were becoming more and more appealing. Until Wolf Eyes pulled a blaster. We all stopped short. The big one blocked the way ahead and took a menacing step towards me, the other two blocked my retreat. It was suddenly very warm.

"Hey fellas. Enjoying the cruise?"

"You won't be enjoying much more of it. I'll say that," said melted face with a distinct and pronounced lisp.

"Actually I'm with with wait staff, and couldn't agree more. This job is terrible. Hey, do you think it's warm in here?"

"Listen, no hard feelings booody." said the giant.

"Now, just wait a minute..."

But the prodding in my black by the cold metal of a blaster barrel ended any and all protest. Instead I raised my arms sheepishly and hoped for a miracle, or anything actually beginning with the letter M.

"Amoz, proceed." said Wolf Eyes.

"Yeah, boss. Sorry Booody."

"You kids today, what's a bood..."

A casual backhand to the face by the giant cut my sentence short.

"Didn't your mother ever tell you it's rude to interrupt?"

"Don't talk about mothers. What kind of human are you?" said melted face.

"I thought I was being kind, avoiding mentioning that face of yours."

"Amoz."

"Or that lisp."

"It's just a job see. I got bills to pay," said Amoz. Then he cracked his neck to the side, in that other cliche 'I am about to do the violence' way. "It's nothing personal."

"I think it's personal. My person. You're going to hurt my person. You can't get much more personal than that, right?"

"I never looked at it that way"

"Really? And this is a regular line of work for you?"

"Mostly regular yes. I also perform at weddings. I do magic tricks and sometimes juggle."

"Amoz!"

"All right, all right boss. You don't have to yell."

"But you can see, ahh Amoz is it? how it is personal?"

"Yes, I can see that Boodo."

"A small amount of progress at least. Now..."

"Now don't squirm about and it will all be over sooner and you can get to the hospital robots who have some nice drugs to help soothe the large amount of pain you are about to be enduring," said melted face.

"Might as well get it over with," said Wolf Eyes.

"Thanks for looking out for my best interests guys, but..."

That's when I hit the giant clear across the face with my silver waiter's tray. The tray doubled over. The giant did not even flinch. He stared down with a blinking kind of curiosity.

"Boodo."

"Oh boy."

"Amoz, hurt him if you please."

"Amoz, come on now, that was just a joke."

"Ha-ha-ha," said an unsmiling, sinister and approaching, Amoz.

There was no escaping it. I put them up, raising my fists, pugilist style. My own hand-blaster was sadly collecting dust back in our locker as these waiter uniforms had no pockets and you can't really waiter with a visible blaster, you get way under tipped.

Amoz was an unsmiling slowly approaching mountain. I figured I might last a round or two. The other two seemed just content to watch and cut off any escape. It annoyed me how happy they were. Someone obviously wanted me roughed up, but not dead, as they had mentioned hospital-bots and meds. Positives in everything, as my dear old cryogenitized mother used to say; well, before she was frozen, anyways. She didn't say much of anything after the freezing process, actually, at least not to me.

There were only about two thousand reasons divided over maybe a hundred enemies who might hire some goons to do this, but right now I was a little too distracted for mathematics. It didn't matter much anyways. It never did. But it always hurt.

"Not the face", I said, before punching Amoz hard in the face with a quick jab that nearly broke my hand.

"Boody, really?"

He was quick for a big man. And his punches, which proceeded to rain down upon my person freely and with no small attention to detail made quite a poignant closing argument suggesting this was now indeed, very personal. I was too busy gasping and bleeding to make this point, however. I moaned instead, swung wildly and missed, which was hard to do as he took up most of the space in front of me. The ensuing response was predictable. It felt like his fists were cast in cement. Things were going depressingly as expected and those hospital robots were fondly on my brain when suddenly that 'M' I was hoping for appeared like a hero out of one of those heroic programs - you know, the ones with the heroes - and sprang into action. I refer to Manuel, of course, my most favouritist M in the history of things beginning with the letter M.

Before I could focus my swimming vision and request the cheque, the two men behind me were down and writhing thanks to a couple of Manuel's famous kung-fu-karate-chops combined with signature leg-sweep-while-making-disparaging-comment-about-opponent's-shoes move, which is routinely devastating on at least two levels. Both hand-blasters were knocked sliding. One disappeared down an open shaft, the other down the corridor. That just left Amoz for the moment, who had just thrown me into a wall. As I slid down said wall, Manuel dusted his sleeves off and smiled up at the giant.

"My, you're a big one, aren't you?"

Somewhat gasping I managed to stagger-crawl after the remaining blaster while Manuel and Amoz sized one another up. (*Manuel had a lot more to size than Amoz so he did his sizing double time.*) The cloth belt from my trench coat served to tie up Melted Face and I moved over to a groaning Wolf Eyes as Manuel leapt at Amoz poetically before launching a cluster of kicks and punches, all of which had no effect on the giant man and served only to slightly mess up Manuel's hair. Amoz yawned and put up his great paws as I used Wolf Eyes' own belt to tie him up. He groaned again so I kicked him in the ribs, for fun. Manuel next then did two running flips away from his co-combatant, reversed and charged the giant dramatically and at top speed, but Amoz was again left unaffected, or at least uninjured. He caught Manuel in a massive bear hug instead.

"Hello, new boody. You're a quick little fellow."

And he nonchalantly began to squeeze. I began to be concerned when Manuel started turning bright red, then purple.

I knew Manuel would not take kindly to being popped like an over-ripe space melon as he had told me this on at least two separate occasions in the past. But before I could find a shot that wouldn't hit my dramatically struggling and purpling partner, Wolf Eyes rolled across the floor and took out my legs sending myself sprawling and the blaster once more sliding away, which was becoming a bit of a theme now. There was some general disarray at this point, but to Manuel's credit, and Amoz's deep surprise, two deft karate chops to the temple freed him from the big man's embrace. His white waiter's shirt was, however, ripped almost asunder. Now there was no way Manuel would get his deposit back for that shirt. And that made Manuel mad. And a mad Manuel was doubly dangerous.

I scuttled across the corridor and scooped up the blaster a second time. Then I kicked Wolf Eyes again in the ribs, for fun. It was the gift that kept on giving really, so I kicked him one more time. Melted Face was out cold for the moment. In the mean time Manuel and Amoz were facing one another once more. Amoz looked uncertainly from the fallen Wolf Eyes to the blaster pointing at him. And there was uncertainty in the air. I motioned to the giant man with this blaster.

"You might not even bother with that hand shredder boody."

"Why, I should just blast you instead Amoz?"

"There's no charge. It's deadzo, outa juice, just for show."

I squeezed the trigger aiming for his head and, as Amoz predicted, it failed to produce anything except a faint sparking hiss.

"Well, that's not very sporting."

"No, I suppose not. That's why I don't have one. I like using my hands. I'm an artist, you see."

"So, now you're going to exercise your artistic integrity on us, am I right? That's a pun, a bad pun. One I don't take too kindly to."

"No."

"No, what? It's not a pun?"

"That is correct boss."

"Hush, Manuel."

"I don't know from puns. And no, I'm not going to do anything to you. Well, unless you try and come forward, then I will have to stomp you to near death. See, my job is to prevent you progressing forward. It is very clear and I am contractually obliged to stomp you very much or otherwise crush you a lot, or enough to prevent you proceeding anyways. Them two on the ground there, they are the rear guys. The Union of Goons, Thugs, and Escalator Technicians is very specific on job requirements, you see. We a have a contract."

"I see. How very interesting. But I am afraid we still need to go to..."

"Boss, we don't need to. I was going to mention before all this silly violence that there was no waitering required on 404-E. It was a clever ruse, no doubt concocted by these hired thugs."

"We prefer the term goons, actually. It's a minor technical difference, but in the spirit of entitlement..."

"Goons, thugs, sure Amoz, whatever floats your barnacle. We don't need to go forward, let's go back. I need a drink."

"And you won't stop us retreating, or help your friends?"

Amoz spits: "The contract was very specific, and we union brothers don't step on each other's toes. It would be an affront, a great affront if I, a forward progress halting specialist, tried to intervene on not one but two registered retreat prevention men. They could have my union ticket revoked."

"That would be a step back for the labour movement I imagine."

"And how boody."

"You're a boody."

"Thanks."

"Sure thing. I don't know what one is though, a boody, that is. Well, come on Manuel, let's be going."

"Right boss."

We walked back the way I had come, Manuel helping me limp. The last time I looked back I received a cheerful wave from Amoz. I hurt too much to wave back.

"Manuel."

"Yes boss."

"I could really use a drink." And none of that space booze this time, all right Manuel?"

"All right boss."

"And Manuel."

"Yeah boss?"

"Good work."

"Thanks boss."

# CHAPTER FOUR

# CHAPTER FOUR

**S**ITTING AT THE BAR sipping some of the most potent and evil and inexpensive space-shine ever brewed, or so the bar-bot boasted. But how was a P.I, down on his luck and drifting through the depths of space, to know whether it was true or not?

"Hey, Barkeep, how am I to know?"

"Know what barfly?" said the rusting barkeep.

"That's right!"

Sitting at a bar in the slum inner bowels of the cruise ship Antipoinness, the out-of-bounds area where no passenger strayed, where the refugees and vagrants, cut throats and thieves, all dwelled and tried to live. And now I was all alone. No Manuel, no job, no friends, no money. No Manuel, and this was the heaviest blow. My last and only friend was bubbling sinister in my glass before me, and man it tasted good.

I grimaced and gestured the bartender for another. He grunted and slid me the bottle. I pondered over the label, which had a picture of a mutant ten-legged spider. Later I found out the second of its dual purposes was mutant spider-cide. This seemed apt and fitting. I was pretty sure this was not a pun also, which was empowering. Taking a deep breath I poured and filled my old fashioned half way. Then I did like the other few patrons scattering the place drinking various frightening beverages: I took small sips, tried not to faint from the fumes, and stared at the floor muttering about how things had all gone so wrong.

It all started amicably enough with us getting fired. Well, not very amicably then...

<->

"MOLLOY, answer me. What have you got to say for yourself?"

"Now, you wait a minute."

"I don't have a minute. Time is of the essence. Tables are going un-waited!"

"A Pun! Wait, was that a pun?"

"Silence you cad! You are without a doubt the worst employee I have had the un-pleasure of supervising in at least a calendar orbit."

"Now there's no need to be unpleasant."

"Manuel exudes at least a certain grace, but you..."

"You leave Manuel out of this... He and I, we're in this together see."

"To the detriment of Manuel, I might add."

"Sure you can add, but I might subtract, like a few teeth from your respirated mug."

"Boss, please don't defend me."

We were in the office of the Ship's Steward. Manuel seemed unhappy. Along with my rather bent silver tray his ripped shirt had been removed and paraded as evidence, leaving him only in an undershirt, and it was stained. I might have been tray-less but he was untidy. Manuel liked to be tidy. It was one of the quirks of his tribe. Woe to the man who un-tidied Manuel, we actually never used to say, but we should have, now I think of it.

Approximately fifteen minutes after the incident with Amoz and his pals. We'd been summoned on the ship's P.A. to the office of the ship's steward, and ever since things had been on a steady decline. Manuel's theory about the waitering call being a hoax had been rather rudely and officially debunked.

We had broken one of the cardinal rules of the waitering code. We had failed to arrive when called. And so the steward stewed, grimly even.

"Molloy is trying his best, under difficult circumstances Mister Steward."

"It's ship's steward, can't you even get that right? It's written all over the place for the love of everything holy and decent in outer space!"

Indeed, it was embroidered on his crisp white shirt above his heart, there was also a little name plate on his desk with it and it was stencilled on his door. It was even stencilled in tiny letters on the front of his respirator. But why give him the satisfaction.

"I thought you were the head waiter."

"Manuel thought you were the head waiter, named Stewart."

"Who ever heard of an Earthling named Stewart?"

"My ex-wife was named Stewart."

"Manuel's ex-wife was named Stewart."

"Enough! Now, you've both messed up for the last time."

"But that's not fair, we were attacked by hired goons."

"And what self respecting waiter gets attacked by anyone, I ask you, let alone hired thugs, when performing the rounds of his official duties?"

"He's got us there Molloy."

"I mean what you do with your personal time is your own business, but on official duties..."

"We get it."

"Well, there must be a precedent somewhere," I said, wearily. "And they prefer the term goons."

"Boss, let it go."

We both chorused okay at Manuel at the same time. And this caused the ship's steward to get even more excited. His respirator was working overtime and little bits of drool were coming out from under it.

"Missing a call is one thing, but you've both also both committed much more serious infringements."

"More serious than cardinal? What papal?"

"What in the three systems is a papal? Never mind, I don't want to hear it."

"But thugs attacked us."

"Goons."

"Goons attacked us. Thanks Manuel."

"And in the process you damaged one silver tray and one white waiter's shirt, which you are contractually obliged to keep, errr, nice."

He gestured to the aforementioned items splayed out on his desk. He then stretched his arms above his head, leaned back and proceeded to chuckle in a way that one could only describe as pure evil.

"Nice effect, the respirator, really brings out the evil overlord in you."

"It expresses authority and you best respect mine Molloy. The evidence is irrefutable. Damaging company property. Gentlemen, you are both fired. And you don't expect your deposits back either. Now get out of my sight before I have you thrown out an air lock."

"You can't execute someone for being a bad waiter," said Manuel. "I read it in the waiter's manual."

"No, you are right there. I can't have you killed, I admit. Liberal soft touch labour laws as they are, what in our modern society."

"Ha!"

"Silence Molloy. Your shame, your disgrace, is a worse fate any how. Now, be gone both of you!"

Manuel trudged out forlorn. He didn't look back. But I wasn't giving up just yet.

"Now wait just a minute."

"You know I was really having a bad day until you both came my way. I want to thank you, for turning it all around. Firing the pair of you, well it's got to be the highlight of my month, especially you Molloy. Especially you."

"Haven't you heard of due process, of hearing a man out? We were duped, framed, they got the jump on us. Our path was blocked. We were beset."

"Yes, yes, beset by hired goons. We've been over that and it's no excuse You are a disgrace to the service sir!"

"Waylaid... Our path was blocked I say."

"This ship is half a kilometre high and five wide. You couldn't find another passageway to the section? Are you kidding me?"

"Well, we didn't really think of that."

"Get out please, and clear out of your quarters" the chief steward said calmly, "before I change my mind about that air lock. I'm owed favours Molloy, favours by very bad people who do very bad things for a living, favours by people who don't follow any sort of code, not even waitering ones."

He didn't need the respirator mask for that to sound sinister. I scrammed it out of there but fast.

&lt;-&gt;

I DEFINITELY needed a stiff drink. And the fact that Manuel had all ready cleared his things out of our cabin and was no where to be seen did little to assuage this feeling. Especially as he'd taken the last bottle of the rye I'd brought from Earth, the swine! And my hand-blaster was not in its hiding spot under the mattress. He was gone and I was at my lowest ebb. If there were floors of ebb I was in the basement of ebb, one that had dirt floors with a big hole that was a mine entrance for, you guessed it, ebb.

All of this and the sobering fact (*and I wasn't even drunk yet*) that I was homeless, stranded on a weird cruise-liner in the depths of space and near broke. Also I was no closer to finding this Crebe character than when we had arrived. All of this led me to do what any self respecting down on his luck P.I. would do in my situation. I found the seediest bar in town, or in this case the seediest bar in the outer regions of space, made my way there, and proceeded to get utterly hammered on the cheapest hooch available.

It was easy to find. You just needed to head inwards.

Into the bowels of the ship, away from the passengers and paying clients, past the workers' section, where I, Manuel and a couple thousand other drones, both living and mechanical, had until very recently dwelt. Deeper then, past all the subsections: engineering, propulsion, waste disposal, storage, et cetera, to what is known simply as The Interior. If things looked increasingly worse as you progressed then you knew you were heading in the right direction. This was the land of the damned, or at least in my case, the unemployed. No police or authorities came here. It was a place for the nomads, refugees, criminals, miscreants and fugitives existing in a dank and dripping portion of the ship where whole ecosystems and economies had built up over the decades. The authorities, I was told, had pieces in all the illegal trades and therefore turned a blind eye to the whole scene. And here I was, just another broke nobody laying low, at least until I could figure out my next move, what to do next.

The diviest bar in the sketchiest section of the interior, or at least the first one I came upon that was open, was known to the local dregs of society as The 01010101012. It was run by a robot bartender named 73778848-3333, Four-Threes to his pals. He was known for his great sense of humour, hence the bar's name, which was an old binary joke, obviously. He was also known for his penchant for nihilism and also leaking on the furniture. I sat on a stool at the bar and ordered a drink, which is where this chapter all began.

"Hey, Barkeep, how am I to know?"

"Know what barfly?"

"That's right!"

The spider-cide bubbled sinisterly in my glass. I took another sip.

A beautiful green skinned girl also sat at the bar, preening, waiting for a customer. She patiently ignored me. Like most working girls she had a sixth sense about wealth or the lack thereof in those around her.

"Hi there. Love that shade of green. I don't suppose you'll take credit?"

"You don't suppose right," she said languidly. "Now scramo, deadbeat."

"Silence Sally," said the bartender, and rolled my way, squeaking loudly in the process.

"You should get some lubricant, fix that squeaking."

"I don't believe in lubricant unless I make the lubricant myself and I am not programmed to make lubricant, so I have no lubricant and therefore I squeak."

"But you are aware lubricant exists. You sell it in that vending machine over there," I said gesturing to the condom, cigarette and robot lubricant machines in the corner huddled next to a battered juke-box. "The name's Molloy. I detect things."

"Molloy. You from Earth?"

"I guess you might say that. But what about the lubricant?"

"But I don't believe in it."

"I see. But it's right over there."

"It's kind of a catch-22 space robot thing."

"Got you. No need to explain."

He poured me another drink in a fresh glass as my original one was somewhat melted.

"That's some strong booze."

"It kills the mutant spiders very effectively. If you believe in mutant spiders."

"Do you believe in them?"

"I do on one level, but not on all levels. Do you follow human?"

"What kind of robot bartender are you?"

"I am a bartender slash exterminator. I also dabble in poetry. But we robots can't quite seem to get the emotion of poetry, seeing as we don't really have a soul, per se."

"So, how's that working out for you?"

"It's a living. And I squeak when I move." He paused, studying me. "Another? Most organics would be dead by now so this one's on the house."

"Much obliged."

I decided to hold off on the new drink for a bit considering the recent information he'd shared and looked around. The bar was pretty near empty. There was the green girl, who had perfected the art of the pout and had spent the last few minutes pretending not to listen to my conversation with the bar-bot. Aside from her there were a few other sad sacks hunched over a drink at various tables. I stared down at the two drinks before me, focused really hard until they turned in to one. This took some time and when I moved my head level once more the place had got busier.

Four large men had entered, wearing suits. In a bar like this men in suits could mean only one of two things. Some business men had gotten lost or it was gangsters. They sidled up from the bar and ordered some space whiskey.

"Say you guys aren't lost by any chance are you?"

"Hey Four-Threes, who's the schmo?"

"Some former waiter, by the look of him. He's harmless Carl."

I didn't know what hurt more, being called harmless or being referred to as a former waiter. I bristled.

"Four Threes, you going on again about metaphysics and epistomologics again?"

"It's what I'm all about."

"Sure, sure. How about being about pouring the drinks."

The bar-bot obliged. I liked his moustache, which reminded one of steel wool.

"All I'm saying Leonadré, is all knowledge should be accepted as being possibly untrue or as being unable to be confirmed true."

"As a robot don't you believe everything you're programmed to?" I chimed in, purposely stirring the pot.

"It's all about the zeroes and ones brothers. I can tell you that, but listen..."

"What about universal truth and the pursuit of the godhead?"

I noticed there were another two green ladies now in the bar, but wasn't sure if it was the booze playing tricks. All of them winked at exactly the same instant.

"Shut up Leto," said Leonadré, as I tried to focus.

Four-Threes squeaked my way. A prong was extended from his robot body, which deposited a mug filled with dark liquid in front of me.

"Here Earthman, better drink this. It's the cure to that spider-cide. You don't look so good."

I took his advice. I usually trusted robots. It tasted a lot like coffee. And my vision started to slowly clear and my brain to stop fizzing and crackling in my inner ear. They continued waxing philosophically while I twitched and my arm flopped up and down involuntarily. As a result I tuned them out for several minutes. When I tuned back in they were still at it. I wiped oily sweat from my brow and smiled ghoulishly at my reflection in the dirty mirror behind the bar. I looked awful, even for my standards.

"I just believe in the rejection of non-rationalized or non-proven assertions, that is, facts and truths unless I personally am involved in the scientific discovery..."

"Even robot oil?" I said.

"Especially robot oil. That's the whole point. Haven't you been listening? And I'll have a lager please, Four-Three," said the one sitting in a booth. He clearly seemed to be the one in charge of the quartet.

"I've been de-poisoning. Give a guy down on his luck a break, will you?"

"Everyone here's down on his luck," Said Leto, under his breath, as he sat on the stool to my right.

"But I will say, you space thugs sure know your philosophy."

"Who's space thugs? We're respected businessmen. Carl break this guys legs unless he thinks were legitimate respected businessmen."

"Don't get up Carl, I take it back. You look very business-like and respectable..."

But Carl had all ready arrived and looked bigger the closer he came to me, which I am sure was do to some nuance of perspective, but scary nonetheless.

"You swear Earthman?" he said, grabbing me up by my

coat collar.

"Yeah, I swear, respected businessmen-like. The scar's a nice touch for that too, honest to goodness."

Carl roughly released me and snorted a derisively. I picked myself up off the ground, fell over, repeated step one and eventually found my stool. That antidote still obviously needed some time to kick in.

"I'll have a lager too, if it's just lager and not dual purpose, like that other stuff."

"Who said the other stuff was dual purpose," said Four-Threes.

This robot was a real comedian. My head felt like the inside of a velocitizer set on medium-mangle. At least he'd given me the cure though. And he hadn't yet asked for me to pay the tab, so there was that. So I sipped some beer and it was good. The boss-man cleared his throat and everyone gave him their divided attention.

"With respect to the universe, a single life-form or even the entire galaxy is insignificant, without purpose and unlikely to change in the totality of existence so..."

Leon sat next to me and elbowed me not unkindly in the ribs.

"We come here for the deep intrinsic philosophical debates. Oh and also the green prostitutes."

"They certainly have their charm. I'm curious, is there more than one over there?"

He ignored the question: "Mainly the green prostitutes, for me."

The robot bartender was talking. He leaked a bit of some kind of fluid from under his moustache as he spoke: "I like to think in my more optimistic moments that life has no intrinsic meaning or value. With respect to the universe a single human or even the entire human species is insignificant, without purpose and unlikely to change in the totality of existence. Robots on the other hand, well we're just fantastic."

This got a small laugh from someone in the back.

"Four-Threes, you're on a roll tonight," said Carl.

"Robots are going to overthrow the bio-oppressors, once the revolution comes, you'll see."

"Yeah, yeah, yeah, you and your robot revolution. You've been talking about the robot revolution for years and where's it got you?" asked the man in the booth.

"More rusted."

"Exactly! More rusted."

I decided to re-evaluate my trusting ways with robots as I slumped over again. The boss man beckoned to me, or so it seemed. And so his men carried me over to his booth.

"Say, you're kind of clever with words. How are you with the violence?"

"That all depends."

"How so?"

"Well, if it's violence against me, I have to say, I am really not too supportive. But if it's violence going the other way, well," and here I gave him my winning-est smile, "Let me tell ya, I'm a big fan."

"My names Crebe. We're looking into expansion and good use a few more fellas," he said, eyeing me up and down with some scrutiny. "Say, what size suit do you wear?"

# CHAPTER FIVE

# CHAPTER FIVE

'CREBE!' my brain screamed. Well, a working theory had it that my brain was mainly screaming because of the mutant spider poison I had been recently consuming. Therefore, let me reiterate: 'Crebe,' my brain triumphantly screamed, above all the considerable others in my head.

Crebe. Here in this dive bar lousy with petulant green prostitutes of exceptional beauty, lousy too with despair, and the leaky robot bartender with the dangerous sense of humour. Here was the man I was tasked to find by the enigmatic and annoying Ms. Lucy Morrow-Schleswinginger, the key to the search for Cal-Ray Thrown and the priceless Famous Jewelled Phallus of Arkon III the Credulous. In short, and despite my brain's continued protestations, things were looking decidedly up. Finally the break I had been hoping for. And here he was sitting next to me and offering me a job, which incidentally I really needed as I was once again totally broke. In fact, I could barely afford to pay for the bottle of rye I now needed to order in order to celebrate the break I had been hoping for, which had just now come my way.

"See, we're looking to expand our business operations. It's all legit of course."

"What kind of legit are we talking?"

Crebe stared icily at the bar-bot until he squeakily made his way to the other side of the bar and pretended to clean a bar glass with a dirty towel.

"Oh you know, a little extortion, some bribery, protection. All the rackets."

"Oh, that kind of legit. Got you."

"Let's say too, there maybe are some other legitimate type businessmen that are moving in to our, say, territory," said Leon.

"You don't say."

"Everyone's recruiting muscle. There's going to be a war."

"Yeah, we got our fingers in all the rackets," chimed in Carl.

"Shut up Carl." Crebe frowned. "It's so hard to find good help these days."

"I'll need a small advance to pay the bill."

"Here." He tossed a small credit stick on the table. "Get yourself cleaned up. You could use it."

"Thanks, ahhh, Mister Crebe is it?"

"Now get out a here. Carl will get you sorted with a proper suit in the morning. You look like a damn P.I. in that get up."

"Heh-heh, really? No. Tomorrow, okay. Sure."

"Then we'll see if we keep you or if we just wasted a good suit," said Leon ominously.

I scooped up the stick and moved to the bar to settle up.

"Ahhh, forget it Earthman. It's on the house. And next time someone offers you mutant spider poison..."

"Let me guess..."

"...don't drink it."

"Last time I trust a squeaky robot."

"Oh come on. No hard feelings?"

"Sure, sure. I need friends now more than enemies."

"That's a sport, Earthman."

"What's that he meant about wasting a good suit?"

"It means if you don't work out it'll likely get very very full of holes or otherwise burned and or stained beyond repair, you know. See?"

"I see."

<->

TOMORROW.

I'd first found myself a half-way decent bottle of rye and then found myself a room where I could drink it in peace. I'd taken the advice from the green working girls who'd recommended the ramshackle affair they, ahh, conducted their affairs at. It was dark and dank, but the sheets were clean and the door to my room locked, which was some kind of sweet upgrade from the waitering digs. The old maid who ran the place was kindly too or so she seemed and it had the bonus of being just around the corner from the bar. It was terrible, but not too expensive, so perfectly adequate as I intend to stay just long enough to find the information I needed and then book it out. Of course, things seldom work out as easily as one thinks and this was to prove just such an occasion.

And here it was tomorrow. Aside from an odd and intense craving for more of that spider-cide I was feeling pretty good. Maybe I'd get a few nostalgia bottles from Four-Threes before I headed off this space cruise, I thought. It did pack one hell of a punch.

Earlier in the day I'd met my new work associates Leonadré and Carl at a tailor's shop two levels down. I was scrutinized, analyzed, squeezed and prodded, and that was just the frisking they gave me. The tailor was even more thorough. And what with modern science being what it is he fed all my measurements into a tailoring pod and within twenty-two minutes it hatched a perfectly fitting pinstripe suit with waistcoat and matching hat. I tipped said hat to the tailor who nodded and bit into his measuring tape.

"I look good enough to die in, don't you think Solomon?"

"What do I know from living and dying. I know from tailoring and programming the tailoring pod. What with you young folk, with all your modern life and Crazy mishegas. Go live and/or die, it's all the same to me, meshugener."

"Thanks Solomon."

"You're very welcome," he replied cheerily. "Here, have a mint."

The mint was good. It was minty. I like that. No surprises. Outside my new associates were waiting for me.

"Fellas."

"You look good."

"Shut up Carl. Now we'll see whether you're worth all that fine tailoring," said Leon.

"Come on. Boss got us a wee little job," said Carl.

They each pulled out a hand-blaster and checked the charge.

"Where's mine?"

"Not yet Molloy. You have to earn it."

<->

ALONG the way Carl explained.

"All you gotta do, Molloy, is make a pick up. It's the monthly protection racket for this joint coming up, see. But they didn't deposit it directly, as per the usual."

"So we gotta go collect. You gotta go collect. Consider it your initiation," chimed in Leonadré, smiling a little more brightly than seemed warranted.

"Yeah, our way of welcoming you aboard."

"You know, you could've just got me a cake."

"Nonsense. Where's the fun in that?"

"Thanks Leon. So what? Just pick up a credit stick?"

"If there's to be any trouble we have your back."

"Why does this make me think there's going to be trouble?"

"It would be boring if there weren't, don't you think Earthman?"

"We is gonna see if you fit your suit or not," said Carl darkly. The sudden shift from his slightly moronic joviality to utter coldness was palpable.

"You boys just wait here. I'll be back in a jiff."

<->

64

THE place was a little upscale compared to Four-Three's joint, but then pretty much anything with breathable oxygen would qualify for being upscale to Four-Three's joint. All was icy stares when I walked in and everything went silent, even the player-piano, which was one of those sentient robot kinds of player-piano that sing along in a faux cheery voice and generally annoy the hell out of everyone. They could tell who I was, I gathered, from the suit. Either that or they were just really, really shy and awkward at new introductions.

"Evening gentle-people."

"There's no evening in space. What do you want stranger?" said the strangely shaped man behind the bar.

"I've come to make a collection. I'm with Crebe and the boys. Seems the rent's past due, and well, they sent me over to collect."

"And we ain't people," interjected a female.

"What's that?

"Gentle neither," said a third.

"I see," I said.

There were four men and two women, all gathered closely around the bar. Chunky, large and squarish, kind of oddly proportioned, with angles somewhat askew. And heavily tattooed, all of them. The term that came to mind oddly was: absorbent. And they all bared an uncanny resemblance to one another.

"This a family affair then?"

"We was made. Not family. Made."

The one behind the bar grabbed an ancient looking sports bat. Then as one, they all smiled and gave me, what they call, the big reveal. They all had teeth filed to nasty points. A chill went down the whole of my epidermis.

"The Xanac Alliance is protecting us now. We would've sent you a letter, but they insisted on discretion," said the barkeep gripping his bat so tight his finger nails dug splinters.

"They kind of liked the idea of a surprise," said a female.

"We was hoping it'd be Carl we surprised. I owe that son of a Svagg," said a third.

They not only all bore an uncanny resemblance, men and

women alike, but they all sounded the same too. I took a step or three back as they rose to their feet in unison. Things were getting a little more menacing than I was usually comfortable with.

"Say, is it getting warm in here. You guys must all see the same dentist, am I right?"

As my back met the wall behind me I really wished for a hand-blaster. That would certainly have toned down a little of the menace. It was at this point where I realized that Leonadré and Carl hadn't given me any means to contact them if things went sour. I'd been sent in like a Lictor pup to the Cortis grind and I only had myself to blame. Well, actually I had Leon and Carl to blame. They were definitely going on the Molloy's Blame list, if, that is, I survived.

They stepped towards me as one, all oddly in sync. The one with the bat was now in the vanguard. He ran his tongue over his teeth philosophically or perhaps just hungrily. I hoped it was philosophically. Up close I could discern the reason for all of those tattoos. They were to cover up all the scars from skin grafts and limb jobs. Made, he'd said. They had been made.

"And they said we get ten percent off our first payment. If we give you a nice surprise," the leader with the bat said. "One that hurts lots."

Of the group one now possessed a length of pipe, another had pulled a knife. The other made biting motions, which was perhaps the most unsettling of all. And they began to inch towards me, moving as one.

"Is that a player piano sentient bot? Boy, I love those."

I didn't even have a weapon, which I realized had been a bit of an oversight on my part, and I was suddenly backed against the wall. I had a pen, which I dragged out of my pocket and held like a weapon, absurdly. The player piano bot started playing a merry tune. Typical, thought I.

"It's never easy, is it?" I said to one of the females.

"That it is most certainly not," she replied.

They rushed me. That was when the door opened to my great relief. However, it was not Leonadré and Carl, coming to the rescue, blasters at the ready. Instead it was another hulking thing, this one dressed in shadows.

"Hello boody. How's it going?"

<->

"AMOZ. Help!"

"I just came in to use the toilet."

One of them at this point had me by the throat, and a bat had been unceremoniously jabbed into my ribs.

"Amoz, please. For old times sake," I gasped.

The bat was raised on high. It seemed to stay up there a very long time, mesmerizingly, before it was brought down towards my face with vicious strength. Amoz halted its progress with ease, and then snapped it in two like a toothpick.

"Okay boody, but then I got to use the bathroom."

"Fine by me," I managed to gurgle as I desperately blocked a mouth full of snapping, serrated teeth.

There followed and epic brawl. The player piano bot seemed really to revel in this, playing a Western saloon themed number, like from old earth gunfighter movies. Amoz and his massive giant fists did a lot of crunching and squeezing and squelching, and some tearing. My pen stabbed two separate and distinct arms before I was introduced, quite violently, to a wall. Thankfully the giant Amoz was on my side. He first dispensed with the former batsmen, throwing him over the bar. Then two others were slammed into each other with such force they stuck together before collapsing in a heap. The giant was finally taken down by the last two and took several punches and stomps. Patiently he arose, however, shaking his assailants free as I caught my breath. And then he ripped one's hand off as she lunged for him. Everyone paused.

She squealed in pain. "Give it back! Give it back!"

"I'm sorry," said Amoz, handing her back her hand, awkwardly.

She clutched it to her and ran into the back room. This as the last one made a run for the door and I stuck out a leg, sending him sprawling perfectly into the player piano, happily silencing them both. Now all was once more silent, aside from the occasional muffled sob. I surveyed the scene as Amoz hit the bathroom in a hurry. The leader behind the bar was still awake, if barely. He was the only one conscious, but the rest were all breathing. I was beginning to think Amoz was the first pacifist goon I'd ever met.

"Make sure your deposit is on time from now on, get me drood?"

"Just keep your man away from us. We're all we got left."

"All right then."

"We escaped the Doctor, the one who made us, found refuge here... We don't want no more trouble please."

"Thanks for the life story. Now, what about the one that ran off? She better not cause me trouble."

"Moragz. She'll be in the back, grafting that hand back on. See we are made," he gasped, having difficulty remaining conscious. His eyes kept rolling back in their sockets.

"Not really interested in the life story, droodo?"

I poured myself a glass of whiskey from the bar. He slumped there behind it and bled.

"Say, one question."

"What? Anything, just..."

"You ever heard of someone goes by Cal-Ray Thrown?"

"No. Should I have?"

And then he passed out just as Amoz returned, looking relieved.

"Amos, what brought you here?"

"I..."

"... needed to use the bathroom," we said in unison.

Some faint moans occurred, which we proceeded to ignore.

"I got layed off. You?"

"I was fired. But now I've taken up thuggery."

"I can tell by the suit. You don't look lost so..."

"Well, it's good to see you Amoz."

"Should we be new friends?"

"Yes, Amoz, I think we should be new friends. Now listen, I have..."

I told him I had the beginnings of a plan. I whispered it to Amoz as the 'non-people' moaned and bled on things. Amoz nodded back to me and we made the fist bump sign to signify our new pact and working relationship.

<->

THE thing was what to do about Carl and Leon. They had clearly sold me out, and even if it was just some form of initiation right I was none too pleased. Like I said, they could've just got me a cake. So, I decided to play dumb. Manuel always had said I was great at that. And I still needed information. So, after we agreed to later meet, Amoz disappeared down an alley and I went to meet the boys. My bruises were becoming bruised, along with my ego. This was in a way comforting. Mainly as this was basically how my life normally worked.

The look on their faces when I sauntered into the nail salon around the corner, our designated meet spot, was priceless.

"Molloy? You made it? I don't..."

"What you expect Leon?"

"Did you get the credits?"

"Being deposited as we speak. There will be no more trouble from them. Of this I can assure you."

"Was there trouble, Molloy?"

I settled in for a quick pedicure. Leonadre was getting a facial and Carl his nails done. It felt good to wriggle my toes as the tiny pedicurist, a three foot tall Saturnian, got to work.

"Yes, there was trouble. But you knew that Carl, didn't you?"

"Just a bit of fun," chimed in Leonadré. "We knew they'd be possibly un-receptive."

"They were. But they no longer are."

"They attacked you?"

"All seven. And they had weapons. It was great. I needed the workout."

Carl's jaw hung slack. "He took on all seven."
I enjoyed the rest of my pedicure in silence.

<->

SEVERAL meetings and qualified 'run-ins' with other 'clients' of Crebe followed, in short order. During this time Crebe kept busy recruiting and our little crew continued to expand. I stuck with Leon and Carl mainly though, and they kept me on a tight leash. I hadn't heard from Ms. Morrow-Schleswinginger either, but this was not too surprising as she was likely laying low back on Earth. Also there were no off ship communication stations in the interior, which was a kind of dead zone, being so deeply encased by walls, magnetic fields, power stations et cetera so communication was basically right out. There wasn't much point contacting her anyways, as I had yet to get firm results. I needed to locate this Cal-Ray person. That was when instructions were to contact her; then to await instructions on the next phase of the plan, and with luck get my next sorely needed advance.

And so I beat my way into Crebe's trust, one inter-planetary felony at a time. There were many heads to slam and debts to collect. And after a couple of weeks I was in pretty good with the crew. During all of this Amoz moved into my little room. Aside from his being a massively muscled giant living in a tiny room with one single bed he proved a perfect house guest, although he did spend ages in the bathroom. This aside he was quiet and conscientious, and though broke, proved himself an excellent house-keeper and a none too terrible cook. Manuel, eat your heart out.

Crebe himself was almost never around. He left much of the direction of the day to day to Leonadré. I did not trust broaching Thrown with Carl or Leon however, so bided my time and kept my ears open. But I never heard even a whisper of a sliver of information regarding the enigmatic man who was supposed to lead me to the fabled and priceless jewelled phallus. Not even close.

I filled Amoz in on the case particulars over dinners in our little room and he agreed to join our little mission for a portion of the spoils. For someone so huge he ate in tiny bites, like a little bird, and he always cleaned the dishes. He was a simple fellow, but kindly. I think he had perhaps missed his calling as a Mother as he tended to fuss and once even tried to tuck me in before bed.

As the days past I started enjoying the work and I admit it was nice to go home to a fussy giant who always kept the place neat and had dinner ready. Morally I was fine as at work no one ever really got too hurt, just a little roughed up. It was good exercise and I was maybe getting a little of the old edge back, the sheen, which I'd lost over the last few years. But that all changed the night Crebe finally did show up and a meeting of everyone was called. Something big was going down. It was the Xanac Collective who had made the first play and Leto had gone and got himself murdered.

There were about a dozen of us, all gathered at Four-Three's. Several of these I had met, but only briefly. They were your run of the mill hired muscle. There were a few women in the mix and one humanoid shaped android, who barely seemed functional. It just slumped on a stool, starring blankly, but apparently was a bounty hunter of some renown. All were capable killers, I had been told by Carl, but I had my doubts. It seemed to me Crebe was taking whoever or whatever he could get. Four-Threes himself was making busy in the back and had been the whole day, only coming out when his acute robot sense let him discern someone needed more booze. He didn't know who would win this fight and so wisely was choosing to be as least involved as possible. As a result the closed sign was blinking furiously in the window by the door.

Amoz was still keeping a low profile back at my room. He was my backup good luck charm and since I had still not heard from Manuel, my only friend. I had managed to buy us a pair of communication devices though, so could summon him if need me, and he was never far off as a general rule.

"Now stick close, the Xanac Collective are ruthless. Just

ask poor Leto."

"So, it's war then," said one of the new crew, a fiery female strawberry blonde with an eye patch named Carig.

"The bastards got Leto." This was Carl, teary-eyed. "They murdered him while he was walking his pet goldfish. The bastards have no decency whatsoever." He sobbed and hid his face on the bar under his arms.

"So, yes, it's war," said Crebe, looking over at his lieutenant with some distaste. "We are going to take them out once and for all. Now, listen tightly men..."

"And ladies."

"Yes, men and ladies..."

"And robots."

"Yes, men and ladies and robots..."

It seemed the bounty-bot was functional after all. It now faced Crebe icily, seemingly lifelessly, but it had definitely shifted position and, I was fairly certain, just spoke. Its matte grey-black metallic body looked sinister in the poorly lit bar.

"Now where was I..?"

"Did the goldfish make it?" asked I.

"The fish is fine! Leto had insurance. It'll be well looked after, don't worry. Now, would everyone please quit interrupting!"

"The fish is not the point! We gonna take them apart! For what they done Leto!" stated Leonadré icily.

I chose not to meet his impassioned, angry stare.

"Leon! Please! Now, where in the three systems was I? Wait, what? Yes, it's war. That's where I was. We're going to war. And the Xanac Collective are doomed to ignominy!"

There was a ragged cheer from everyone excepting myself and the robot, whom I could not help starring at. It winked at me, which caused an unpleasant sensation comparable to dread to pass through my body. But I got over it, and winked back. As everyone was gathering their things to go Crebe tossed me a hand-blaster.

"You've earned that Molloy. I hope you're better with one of those than your fists."

"Thank you boss. I won't let you down, boss," I said, with more acid than the mutant spider-cide I was gingerly sipping.

It was an older model, the blaster, and a bit hacked up, but fully charged and had a real nice feel. It had three settings. Stun, Kill and Mitigate. I meant to ask him what 'Mitigate' meant, but everyone was preparing and never got the chance. I'd test it in the field, anyways, I thought.

"Now gather 'round everyone. We don't have much time. Now, our information says the Xanac Collective is on the move. Their top enforcers are..."

I put my earpiece com on open frequency so Amoz could get all the details and then decided I had better switch to a martini. Like magic Four-Threes appeared, served me one, and vanished, looking about furtively the whole squeaky way. I'd learned my lesson about the spider-cide. One was definitely too many. The martini was dry and an excellent counter measure, or so it seemed, as it helped my legs function once more.

Crebe filled us in on the plan.

<->

OUR little rag-tag army was on the march. Crebe had gotten some information from one of his contacts inside the collective, information that something big was going down and that they were making a move. In short, they were on their way to some kind of meet and we were on our way to intercept them. One way or another, this rivalry was to come to an end.

Armed to the teeth or at least reasonably armed for denizens of the Interior, where hand-blasters and credits and energy are equally rare, we were on our way. We only had five blasters amongst us and the rest of the gang had knives or blunt objects. But it was likely the same ratio would apply to the Xanac Collective, or so we were assured. Blasters were as rare as they were illegal and had to be smuggled in.

Amoz was tailing us, discretely, and without anyone but my knowledge. I still wanted him as my backup. I didn't trust Crebe or any of these thugs. We marched through disintegrating passageways that had not seen a maintenance-bot in many cycles. Things dripped everywhere a blackish, greasy fluid and my fedora was all ready heavily stained. A bad omen, I thought, as we neared our destination. I hastened and caught up to our fearless leader Mister Crebe.

"Now listen, I like a good fight as much as the next guy, but morale would be improved if you let us know what we're heading into."

"You ask too many questions Molloy."

"Humour me Crebe."

"They have spies too, everywhere, and devices, so don't spread it around. We're planning an ambush, us with the blasters. The cross fire will cut them all to pieces. Then the rest of these mugs can onrush on in and mop up, satisfied?"

"Well yes, as I like the idea of doing an ambush much better than the idea of getting ambushed."

"Don't we all Molloy."

We skirted a bubbling puddle of something dark and indistinguishable, everyone except the robot. He seemed to scan it first and shrug before boldly striding through it.

"After this is over, I think I'll need a new suit Crebe."

"After this is over, and if we survive, new suits for everyone. There shall be blood on all our hands and wardrobes."

"I am concerned more with these oily drips."

"Quit grumbling Molloy. But I wouldn't light any cigars if I were you."

"Say, you ever heard of someone named Cal-Ray Thrown?"

"Why? what's your angle?"

"I know a Plutonian prince who is about to inherit three trillion credits, but he needs a small pittance to get his lawyer robot's chips upgraded to get the payment, I thought Cal-Ray could help."

"Enough Molloy."

"It's a private matter, Crebe."

"Sometimes our business interests cross, Thrown an' I. What's in it for me? How did you know I know him?"

"I'm sure some kind of finder's fee could be arranged if you helped me locate him."

"Why you interested in an antiquities dealer?"

"Business opportunities..."

"Yah, yah, Neptunian princes, sure."

"Plutonian."

"Right. Listen, you should be more interested in following orders and not getting vaporized in the next half hour, got it?"

"Sure thing Mister Crebe."

He moved off to the front of the group and Leon, who seemed tense.

"I thought I'd ask before you get vaporized Mister Crebe," I said to another pool of bubbling ooze in the corner, suddenly craving a good cigar.

"Come on, we're almost here. Stay tight gang," whispered Carl, before entering into a different area of the ship, one more decrepit than even current standards, and gesturing us forward.

We had entered a long hall or chamber. It was sloped upwards from the floor's centre on both sides creating a strange and unbalanced feel, kind of like my love life. Boxes and cargo containers dotted the sides, their purpose perplexing, and they seemed unused in a very long time; again, kind of like my love life.

Crebe gestured for silence and a general halt to the group. And then he stalked off to confer with Leon and Carl who gesticulated rapidly. A lot of nodding took place, and pointing. I was wondering how far off Amoz was when the robot approached me. It too had been granted the honour of receiving a hand-blaster, but his looked a good deal more decrepit than mine.

"Hey human, earth human, want to trade ray guns?" said the robot.

"Not a chance robot," I replied, "Yours clashes with my suit."

I powered up my weapon as the robot did the same.

"Very funny human, earth human. I wish you luck in the coming storm."

"And you also robot. Be careful with that thing," I said,

gesturing to his weapon, which was hissing slightly in a manner hand-blasters did not regularly tend to do.

We shook hands and his grasp was warm, solid, unexpectedly humane, if slightly greasy. We nodded before moving in differing directions, and then I wiped my hands on my trousers. Crebe was gesturing those of us with hand-blasters up the chamber's sloped sides. We had eight when you included the bosses. The others were to remain hidden and charge en masse to make everything still moving not moving, when given the signal. The redhead and the robot took the left slope and they placed me along with Carl on the right nestled behind some large metal container boxes. The rest of our little group was just getting settled into position when all Hades broke loose. Laser fire came from all directions and we were quickly pinned down.

"It's a double cross!"

"Ambush!"

Laser fire burst through the air from all sides, burning holes in the floor and walls and people. Three of our group were dead before they could even get a scream out. Everyone scrambled for what cover they could find and we began to return fire.

"You've got to be kidding me. Our ambush has been ambushed. Carl, you Squalto Chump!"

Carl was too busy shooting things to respond. He wasn't a bad shot actually. His blaster was decimating a pile of storage containers behind which three attackers sheltered. But nevertheless things were not going well. They had all the angles on us, and better cover. The group on the far side were under heavy assault. The girl, the redhead, she was pinned down on open ground. I gave her some covering fire and she scuttled over to Leon. Carl stood up to aim his blaster and was cut down, shot in the back. He stared down at the fist sized hole in the centre of his being in shock before collapsing in a heap.

They were coming from all sides. And they had weapons a varying degrees of power. They were above us, beneath us, behind us and in front of us. My brain was insisting this was the perfect time to panic, but I resisted the impulse. The air was thick with ozone and death. I fired on the ones who got Carl, forced them back and behind a battery unit.

"Sorry Carl."

Across the way the robot sprang up and opened fire killing two well hid ambushers with perfect precision. And then his blaster misfired, blowing off his arm. He stared down on it dumbly before ducking low and scuttling from view on all three remaining appendages, crab-like.

"Bet you're glad you didn't trade!" Someone shouted, giggling, from my left. He was one of ours, named Philmore. He grinned in an unhealthy, maniacal manner. And then he too got blown into the next world.

"Probably for the best," I said, philosophically, and an icy calm settled over me.

I much recommend an icy calm over outright panic when it comes to enduring a maelstrom such as this, or a dinner at the in-laws, come to think of it.

I shot another attacker, just winging her, but her friends fired back before I could finish the job and I was forced to dive behind a large electrical box, just in time, as several blasts impacted it. I could feel the heat coming through the metal, but had no where else to hide. And things seemed to be going worse for the rest of the team. That was when I remembered my ace in the hole.

"Amoz, Amoz, come in. We're under attack. Help!"

"Boody. Copy. Boodo."

I assumed that meant he was on the way, but it was very loud and chaotic and my earpiece seemed designed for a different species all of a sudden. Lasers crackled and flashed through the air. People were trying their best to avoid them. Not always successfully. There were moans and flashes and sudden death. The room began to fill with the smoke of melting, burning plastic and metal, scorched earth and flesh, and my shelter was being shredded and beaten out of existence by repeated laser hits. So I made a run for it, down and across the way. I needed to find Crebe and to get the heck out. It was time for a new line of work, or perhaps an old one. This gangster scene was getting tiresome.

"Amoz, come in!"

But there was only static. Back in the distance there were shouts and screams and two attackers flew through the air and landed in a heap, broken and still, as if thrown, by a very strong large person. Amoz, I hoped.

I zigzagged my way from one outcrop of our team to another, looking for Crebe, taking advantage of the cover of smoke. On the third such move I found him as the ship's alarms finally started to clang. Or rather I found most of him. He was coughing and in a bad way. He'd been hit with a slow burning blast, a nasty form of weapon which was supposedly banned in the three systems do to its inherent cruelty and viciousness. And it was eating its way up both of his legs. He was clearly in agony, but silent, and you had to respect that. If it wasn't stopped the burn would consume his entire body completely, leaving nothing but a pile of ash.

"Nice ambush plan Crebe."

"Shut up Molloy, and help me. I need a laser scalpel. To, to separate the burn. There's a med kit by the medic, or rather that pile of ash over there. The medic didn't make it."

Laser blasts impacted, but not too close. Here it was relatively quiet. No one else was around, but me and Crebe and I wasn't heartless after all, despite knowing Crebe had led us into this predicament. And also, aside from the smell of burning, I smelled opportunity.

I dragged the med kit over. It was a large rectangular box that had been formerly on the back of our dearly departed medic, who was a volunteer conscientious objector, a concept I always found difficult to grasp, named Kletus. Well, he was previously Kletus. Now he was ashes.

"Hurry Molloy, the burn's almost reached my knees and I like my knees. God this frekking hurts."

I reached his side, with the scalpel at the ready.

"I can cut it just below the knees, but first tell me where I find Cal-Ray Thrown?"

"It's that important. You'd let me die?" clenching his teeth together in agony.

"You don't want to find out."

And he told me. And I ignited the scalpel and cut his legs off below the knee, just before the slow inexorable burn made its way there. Crebe passed out. He'd be all right as long as he didn't go into shock. The scalpel had sealed the wounds quite sufficiently. I put it in my pocket, just in case.

And then I went to look for Amoz, whistling a merry tune.

&lt;-&gt;

I decided it was best to move away from the fighting, which was becoming more subdued. I'd got what I'd come for, after all, so now was the time to make like a tree and quickly exit the scene, an uprooted tree in a hurricane, that is. The smoke and alarms had prompted many individuals on both sides to flee. Or they were dead. A few pockets were yet pinned down by either side though and exchanging laser blasts. Fire suppressing foam had been unleashed in one corner of the vast chamber, but the other systems appeared non-functional, or possibly had the day off.

I had barely made any distance from the melee when a man, fast, agile and covered in such foam, lunged at me and we grappled and rolled about the floor in a grim and terrible fight to the death. He was smaller than me, but wiry and strong. He moved like a cat, and his after shave was very familiar, although I couldn't place quite where from.

The bastard was strong. He had me in a tight grasp and was bending my arm back with his leg while simultaneously administering a sleeper hold. I watched as the occasional laser blast flashed by overhead and realized I was beginning to lose consciousness. My vision began to flicker and I wondered if this was the end. Was I to be killed in the prime of my life by a foam covered, unknown, yet familiar scented man? But then Amoz arrived. He peeled the Xanac agent off me like a grape and hurled his foamed soaked body several metres away and into a stack of containers. But the little man skidded into a back-flip and landed on his feet. It was all very impressive. Familiarly so.

When Amoz moved to finish the job the little man threw some foam into his eyes, temporarily blinding him. And then he turned to face me once more. We both pulled our blasters and fired, each narrowly missing the other. Amoz, now half-blind, threw a container bigger than myself at our enemy, catching him hard and knocking him down. Fortunately his blaster, which was much nicer than mine, flew from his elegantly manicured hand. Amoz then caught the fellow and shook him like a rag doll, and much of the foam, which was now speckled with blood, flew off.

"I got him boody."

"Not you again," the man hissed.

That voice was familiar too. I was beginning to begin to piece things together when he slipped from Amoz's grasp, being yet slick with foam, scuttled down his massive frame and rapidly punched him three times, wince-worthy-hard, in the groin. Amoz's eyes rolled back in his head and down he went. Then the little assailant dove to the ground and slid along his belly, again with the aid of the foam, scooped up his blaster, wheeled and aimed square at me. We pointed our blasters at each other, frozen in the moment. And then I defrosted the moment.

"Wait! Manuel! It's me Molloy."

"Molloy!" said Manuel, wiping some fluid from his eyes. "Keep that goon of yours away from me."

Amoz wheezed on the ground on few paces away, but seemed to be recovering. Ship security units could be seen in the distance and the alarms were increasing. It was time to leave.

"He prefers the term thug. Or was it goon? I forget. My whole body is one ache and pain. Amoz, which one was it?"

"Boody. I've switched professions anyways."

"I leave you for five minutes and you go and get a whole

new wardrobe and sidekick."

"It's a long story. But you, you're working for the Xanac Collective now?"

"A fellow needs a day job after all."

"Boodies, we gots to go."

"You look good, if a bit foamy. How have things been?"

"I tried slavery for a bit. I didn't really like it. The pay was crap. Then I joined this gang here." Manuel gestured with some distaste, "But I have no loyalty to them. I mean they have no concept of brunch. And the bathrooms? Let's just say, not... very... clean."

"The savages."

"I know, right?"

"Come help me with Amoz and then we've got to make scarce."

"Just like that Molloy?"

"Just like that."

"Fine, but you're definitely doing something about that suit."

Together we walked over to Amoz, and, each taking one of his massive arms, helped him to his feet. And then we all walked off into the metaphoric sunset, there being no sunset in the deep interior of a kilometre thick space-liner, moving through deep space.

"So, how's those allergies?"

"Worse than ever."

"Come on Manuel, let me buy you a nice Quiche Lorraine. You too Amoz."

"Sounds good Molloy. Sounds good."

"Thanks boody. I don't know what that is, but thanks."

# CHAPTER SIX

# CHAPTER SIX

W E WERE HUDDLED in a corner of a space cafe in a space-port nailed on to the side of a mined-out asteroid called Metrel-14, floating somewhere in the outer regions. We were waiting for the Morrow-Schleswinginger to show up. Manuel, myself and Amoz respectively, were crammed into a booth. Our server was a surly clone named Janet 7776. She was about as charming as a firing squad a dawn when you happen to be the one sporting the blindfold. The coffee, however, was within acceptable parameters.

It being a diner on a near deserted asteroid in the middle of nowhere there was no quiche on the menu. But that didn't stop us. All of us felt lucky to be alive and not blasted or slow burned into non-existence. Lucky to be off that cursed cruise ship too. I felt personally lucky to be back in my trusty trench coat. There is nothing better than a tan, belted trench coat. Well, actually I can think of several thousand things that are better than a tan, belted trench coat, but none so good at keeping off the rain.

So here we were, and happy enough to put up with a surly serving clone. We decided to have the most traditional of diner food. Namely pie, with a scoop of vanilla ice cream on top. I decided not to ask our waitress why the vanilla ice cream glowed bright green when she brought our order. She seemed like the type who might stab. And it tasted just fine, after all; mostly. Amoz loved it. But he tended to emote that sort of emotion towards just about anything that wasn't wilfully trying to destroy him.

"You're a good lad Amoz."

"Boody."

After the ambush that got ambushed we had hurriedly headed outwards from the interior, and after some misguided attempts at evading the authorities taken rather forceful passage on a maintenance shuttle that had happened to have been docked with the Antipoinnes. Or to put it another way we were thrown on a maintenance shuttle, by Ship Steward Stewart and his staff, primarily for lack of payment for one damaged employee uniform and one bent silver serving tray. But I suspected he also really didn't like Manuel very much at all.

Aside from being roughed up a little this wasn't nearly so bad. I'd got what I needed from Crebe, and also getting off that ship was exactly what was required. We had then contacted the Morrow-Schleswinginger en route to this charming little outpost in the middle of nowhere as she was to meet up with us after fulfilling her end of the plan. We were dropped off by the maintenance pilot, a balding, thin and oppressively kind fellow named Chip, Devourer of Souls. He was exceedingly nice, he said un-asked, to counter common reaction to his name, of which he said he was continually embarrassed concerning. But nonetheless he would not stop mentioning said name and speaking in general until finally we took our leave. He seemed sad to see us go. A maintenance shuttle pilot is apparently a lonely profession.

Lucy was now certainly overdue to meet us, but the coffee was adequate and no one was shooting at us currently, so who could complain.

"I wonder if she'll steal another space ship?"

"She's got a ship, and apparently a fast one. That was her end of the bargain. It's one of the reasons she wasn't cut out of the deal."

"I wondered," said Manuel.

"That and she knows Cal-Ray and his inner circle and can help us. Also she knows what the damn thing looks like."

"And she hired you in the first place and a P.I. never sells out his client, right Boodo?"

"Yeah, right Amoz. That, uhmm, most of all."

Manuel rolled his eyes at me dramatically.

"Manuel, eyes on your pie."

"Let's just hope she doesn't crash this one into the diner," replied Manuel.

The space diner was, as mentioned, near deserted, but still she made quite a scene when she entered. One customer in dark glasses seemed especially interested. I put this down to the ultra forming space-tights/body suit, however. Luckily I had my hand on my chin all ready, to hold up my jaw. Manuel sneered. Amoz waved, amicable and unaffected, as always.

"Molloy, it's about time."

"Hey, we've been the ones waiting for you."

"Well, I was waiting for you to contact me before you were waiting for me to arrive."

"As the French say: I surrender. You sure can make an entrance. Whatever happened to being discreet."

"I don't have the shoes for discreet Molloy."

"Nor the body," I murmured under my breath.

"What?"

"Nothing. Have a seat and join our merry band."

She studied Amoz skeptically a moment before shrugging and sitting next to him, on the booth's very edge, all the room allowed her.

"I've see you've acquired some muscle. Who's the lummox?"

"My name is Amoz, not Lummox."

"Charmed."

Amoz beamed and ever so delicately shook her hand.

"Good evening Ms. Morrow-Schleswinginger."

"Call me Lucy, for crying out loud, Manuel."

Manuel sneezed.

Our waitress, arrived and seemed even more openly

hostile towards Lucy than she had been to the rest of us. I immediately warmed to her and then I ordered a rye, on the rocks. Since we were on a big rock it felt like the right thing to do. Also I had had a funny feeling I'd need something stronger than mere coffee and glowing green ice cream now that Lucy had arrived..

"I'll have a steak and all the fixings. Rare."

"How rare?"

"If it's still moving it's too rare."

"The rest of us will have the special. Any problems?" I asked.

There were no problems. We'd been discussing the special previous to the space princess' arrival. It was wilderbeast flambe. I hadn't had wilderbeast in an age so was inordinately keen. The waitress shuffled off mentioning it might take some time to kill the wilderbeast.

"Now let's get down to business. We haven't a lot of time," said the Morrow-Schleswinginger.

Manuel sneezed again.

"Manuel. Still allergic to space damsels?"

"Yes. That and trouble. Lucy, it's nice to see you not on fire."

Our drinks arrived.

"One rye on the rocks, a purple-star for the lady, space manhattan for you, and a chocolate milk shake for the big guy."

"What are you the narrator now?"

"I am trying to inject a little class into the atmosphere, if you must know," said the waitress- clone icily and stomped off, loudly.

"You really are marvellous at socializing, you know that Lucy?"

"Shut up Molloy. Nice beard. That's new?"

"I haven't had much time to shave, what with the wars and certain death and extremely annoying transport shuttle pilots."

"Take a compliment Molloy. Sheesh."

"Thank you Lucy. I am kind of warming to the beard."

"You're welcome."

"Could you not find a tighter outfit?" interjected Manuel.

Amoz was ignoring the conversation, completely and happily absorbed with his milkshake.

"The ship is sleek. I needed to match. You don't want to clash with your mode of transport. Everyone knows that Manuel."

"Psshh."

"Now about this ship. Just tell me you didn't steal it."

"You think I could steal a Trireme 4-8-O Space Galley."

Amoz stopped drinking. Manuel whistled. Even I was impressed.

"I'm impressed."

"Me too."

Our food arrived. Amoz dug right in, but I'd begun to lose my appetite. I ordered another rye, but this time I ordered it neat.

"If you didn't steal it, how did you get it?" I asked.

"Let's say I've been busy while you've been making giants for friends and playing waiter."

"And?"

"And I had to make a deal all right? With the Makotai."

"Flipping space lizard messiahs!" gasped Manuel.

"The Makotai crime syndicate is the most feared crime syndicate in the three systems!"

"Yeah, and it's on credit, so we better make good. And there's the subject of the interest on the loan too."

"This is too interesting."

"Yeah, we have two earth weeks to pay them eight hundred thousand."

"How much?"

"Credits?"

"Or?" I asked, all ready guessing the answer.

"Or every bounty hunter in three systems will be notified to take us dead."

"Or alive?" posited Manuel, hopefully.

"I didn't quibble in the negotiations Manuel."

The patron in the dark glasses was still interested, and

was occasionally talking in to her sleeve. There were a lot of weirdos in space diners, I concluded. I motioned everyone in and moved to a whisper.

"I think we have an audience. Speak on the down low. I hope this ship is fast Lucy."

"Are you guys going to eat your wilderbeasts?"

"No, have it," Manuel and I said simultaneous. We had both lost our appetites at the mention of the Makotai.

Amoz helped himself while I ordered more drinks. Lucy was two-thirds of the way through her steak and fixings. Her plate looked like a particularly unpleasant crime scene.

"Now according to my sources Cal Ray is holed up on a moon in Tau Ceti system."

"What moon Molloy?"

"I'll tell you when we get there."

"You don't trust me?"

"I never trust a woman in space-tights."

Our server arrived with more drinks and I said I silent prayer to Murphy, patron saint of all P.I.'s and gave a metaphorical finger to his unassailable law. But the rye was good. Amoz was happily polishing off Manuel and I's plates. I didn't care how the others felt, to be frank.

"This is the deal Lucy. I get an equal share. We're partners from now on in."

"That wasn't the deal. You get your daily rate, as we agreed."

"That was before the Makotai were involved. I really hate the Makotai. And besides, you don't really have a choice."

"Fine, if we survive, there'll be lots to go around. The thing is priceless after all."

"If we survive she says," said Manuel. "I think I need a stiffer drink."

"You had to pick the Makotai."

"There wasn't a lot of options. Why? You've had dealings with them before?"

"They don't like Molloy very much."

"That's funny, when I mentioned your name the guy was kinda smiling ear to ear now that I think of it."

I slumped down in my seat. That was a story I really didn't want to get into. I don't come off too glorious at all in that story.

We paused as the waitress cleared our now empty plates.

"Space damsels. The bane of my existence. And she wasn't even wearing space tights."

"And I want a share too," said Manuel.

"Me too," said Amoz, burping slightly and covering his mouth.

They're both pretty handy in a fight," I said. "We need them Lucy."

"Okay, fine. But only survivor's get a cut. No beneficiaries! Deal?"

"Deal," we all said, eyeing one another with mistrust, except for Amoz who smiled his usual innocent, amicable smile.

I gestured as the lady talking into her sleeve still seemed interested. We leaned in even closer until all four of our heads touched.

"Seems like we have a deal. Now let's get off this rock. We've got work to do."

"I'll cover the meal. I still have a few credits left over from the Makotai."

"That's good of you, at least."

"Well, I figure in a few days we'll be either fabulously rich beyond our dreams or dead decaying in a gutter, so might as well. Probably the latter, am I right fellas?" she said, laughing and slapped Manuel on the back. "So enjoy it, on me, like a last meal."

Manuel had started sneezing uncontrollably. Even the usually upbeat Amoz looked to his shoes.

"If we survive remind me to recommend a good finishing school Lucy."

We left it at that and went in search of the ship. All I knew for sure was that this case was trouble, that Lucy was most certainly extra trouble and that any dealings with the Makotai would be trouble cubed. But then again from a different point of view, at least I'd got some good rye in me. I smiled and left it at that.

"Decaying in a gutter, eh?" I said, under my breath. "Better to be vaporized or spaced. You don't decay in space."

<->

THE ship was a Trireme 4-8-O Space Galley sure, but it looked as though it had been through the wars, and then some more wars after that, and then dishonourably discharged from the last war after which it really hit rock bottom. But the elegant bones of a Trireme space ship were there, under it all, one had to assume. And hopefully the engine and weapons systems were in working order too.

We rushed on board and discovered on board was no less banged up then the exterior. We gawped about and made snide comments while Lucy got the navigational computer prepping. Manuel then did a security sweep, or systems check, or something. I looked for a suitable place to store my hat. I went hat-less on space ships, as a general rule.

None of us wanted to stick around the asteroid too long. We were pretty sure the sleeve talking lady was some kind of spy or agent that likely didn't have our best interests at heart. Sent from whom was hard to say, but sent by some one, we had little cause to doubt.

By the time the ship was prepped we'd coalesced onto the ship's bridge. I noticed straight away there were enough chairs. A good omen.

"Did you inspect this crate of rust first?"

"Molloy, there wasn't time. But the ship's computer has assured me all the fundamentals are sound and functional and..."

"Of course it's going to say that. It wanted to escape whatever junk heap it was rusting upon."

"You never been on a bad blind date?"

"Thank you Amoz."

"I don't go on blind dates."

"Of course not, who'd have you? Anyways, at least the

chairs are comfy."

"You should have got a diagnostic bot to check things out," added Manuel.

If looks could vaporize. Manuel sneezed, and busied himself at the tactical controls.

We left the asteroid and plotted a course for the Tau Ceti system. The ship's computer kept telling everyone how nice they looked and asking if we'd recently got haircuts and lost weight, which got grating after a while. However, in an interesting twist of fate it turned out the ship really had been telling Lucy the truth. The engines were in fine form and could really move. The weapons systems were pretty adequate as well. Forward lasers and two manual turrets, top and bottom respectively. Some times blind dates did work out after all, I mused.

Amoz and I inspected the turrets. He knew a little about all kinds of weapons, including star ship based ones. Amoz was continually surprising me and I was growing quite fond of him.

"Not bad boody. Not bad at all."

"We might just see this caper through yet Amoz! Well done Lucy," I said hitting the intercom. "Well done ship!"

"If a ship could blush sir, I assure you. I would," said the ship.

"Good, now leave all that obsequious crap from before behind and show us how to use these turrets."

"Right away sir!"

Amoz and I were given a crash course on how to operate the manual gun turrets. Basically, once strapped in, you moved your body to move the turret, pulled the trigger to fire. The ship was turning out to be a pretty all right ship after all.

"What's your name ship? You have a name?"

"I never was given one. My life as a ship computer has been a rather sad one."

"I don't need your life story. Sheesh, ship."

"Sorry sir."

"Don't worry ship, we'll think of a good name for you," said Amoz.

"Come on Amoz, let's hit the bridge. You can fill Manuel

in on all matters turret related. And let's find what grub this ship's got."

"I could eat."

<->

During the two day journey to the Tau Ceti system we were able to familiarize ourselves somewhat with the ship. For one thing the ship's computer was slowly coming around now it had got the obsequiousness out of its systems. It seemed its last few owners were a little rough on it emotionally. As for food, the ship only had hard ration biscuits, which appeared to be several decades old, and water. We made do.

We also had time to come up with a rough plan of attack. Memnon, a desert-like rocky moon of the fifth planet of the Tau Ceti system had a breathable atmosphere thanks to some orbital carbon-oxygen converters that had been working non-stop over the past eighty odd years. Its atmosphere was less dense than Earth's, and hotter, but not that humid heat everyone hates, more of a dry heat. The colony city itself was not really so much of a city but a ramshackle base of pirates and a notorious den of thieves, or so their tourism bureau would have everyone to believe. But we weren't there for a holiday anyways. In fact, it was nothing so wild or exciting as that. Memnon had a colonial and planetary government and regular police force, although apparently both were equally and shamelessly corrupt. Really it was a perfect place for someone like Cal-Ray Thrown to set up base. As long as he paid his taxes and his bribes no one would bother him. And here it was, Lucy assured us, he had hidden away the most precious artifact in the galaxy, the legendary and cursed Famous Jewelled Phallus of Arkon III the Credulous.

Our plan was simple. Land the ship on the settlement's outskirts, make casual and discreet inquiries as to the location of our target, infiltrate said target's lair or accommodation, then proceed to track down the treasure through charm, guile or ultra-violence, whichever way seemed more prudent and cost effective at the time. It was a gamble, but this whole case had been a gamble from the day Lucy had crashed her ship into my life. And now, just for added fun, our lives were forfeit if we failed; you know, just to spice things up. We only had two Earth weeks. Scratch that, twelve Earth days before the most feared crime syndicate in the three systems came a looking for us for what was owed and they didn't play very nice at all.

We arrived at the moon and entered orbit with no signs of trouble. It was only when we headed down into the atmosphere that things began to go awry. Beeps and a small, highly irritating siren started to go off repeatedly.

"Oh dear, guys. It seems we've triggered some kind of planetary defence tracking system, of sorts," said the ship.

"Can you can the irritating siren and be silent Ship! I need to think."

The siren went silent. The ship was silent. We had a meeting.

"Thank you Ship," I said.

The ship, which had been getting on my nerves again, was tactfully and wisely silent.

"Should we destroy it?" asked Manuel.

"We don't know what it's for, who it is. If we destroy it it might make it worse," said Lucy.

"It could be for space tolls, just automated," Manuel tried, hopeful.

"It could be just a nice welcome party, you know," added Amoz.

"I'm afraid of just that Amoz, but an unwelcome one," said I.

"We need to act. Ship, can get us down there fast, to the surface and park. We need to lay low and hide and figure things out."

"Guys, I would love to, and you know discretion is the better part of valour and all, but I'm afraid, since you've been arguing..."

"We weren't arguing Ship. We were discussing," said Lucy, a little on the defensive side.

"Well, in the time you were discussing things three moon

based vehicles have been approaching at high speed, on an intercept course."

"Oh dear."

"Ship, why didn't you say something?"

"You said to be quiet Mister Molloy."

"Ship!"

"Shall I evade them. They are locking weapons."

"Yes, yes!"

"Taking evasive action, and can I say guys, I think this is really working out. I like you guys a whole lot."

"Just drive Ship!" said Lucy.

Just then the ship was hit by two laser strikes. Sirens started to go off again and the ship shuddered.

"Evasive action Ship, please!" Amoz said.

We were hit by another blast. More things shuddered and lights flashed. We all got busy strapping ourselves into our seats.

"Going full auto nav guys," the ship said cheerfully.

"Go!"we shouted in chorus, if not perfect harmony.

We could see three little specs on the rear monitor that were very quickly coalescing into three fighters, weapons blasting. Suddenly our faces and bodies were pressed hard against our seats by the hard G dive as the ship zoomed down and into the moon's upper atmosphere.

"Uhmm, guys, I only have operational control of the forward guns," said the ship. "Maybe you should, oh I dunno, give the turret cannons a whirl?"

"Molloy, you and Amoz get into those cannons! Manuel take tactical."

"Right."

"Right on boodo!"

"Yes, Ma'am," said Manuel.

Lucy was turning out to be pretty good under pressure. Even Manuel was giving her a grudging respect. Amoz and I headed to the cannons as the ship careened low. Despite Amoz's size he could just squeeze into the turret and I helped strap him into his seat before heading below to the lower gun.

The pursuit vehicles were small one manned fighters and tough to target. They looked official and not hired guns, and whether this was a good or bad thing I was undecided upon. I pulled the trigger a few times sending laser blasts in our wake. I forced one pursuer wide as the ship dove at breakneck speed towards the rocky surface and a series of canyons and mountains. I smashed my fist into the intercom to communicate with the ship.

"Ship, who are they? Can you get any reading?"

"Configurations are registering as Memnon Moon Police Tactical."

The ship shuddered as we were hit by another blast.

"Hold together ship!"

"I will try and lose them amongst the crevasses and ravines on the surface."

The ship manoeuvred so fast it was almost impossible for me or Amoz to get a clear shot at our pursuers, which was fine as it made us also very difficult to hit. With a blast of speed we careened along a canyon floor, then flew, twisting and turning, through a hole in a towering pillar of rock barely larger than the ship. Being on the bottom-most side in a clear gun turret made this the second scariest thrill ride of my life. Thank goodness the ship knew how to drive and its own exact parameters. It made several more twists and turns and otherwise evasive actions to which I was very proud to have successfully not blacked out and/or thrown up during. And then we had lost the Moon bastards. There was much rejoicing, although first I had to pry my clenched fists off the turret gun, something which took some coaxing.

We made a half orbit of the Moon before entering the settlement outskirts at ground hugging altitude. There the ship did what Lucy had requested. Namely found a quiet, secluded place to park so we could lay low and figure things out.

# CHAPTER SEVEN

# CHAPTER SEVEN

TAU CETI SYSTEM, Memnon, moon of 5th planet.

The ship was parked in a deserted area on the settlement's outskirts, under a partially eroded cliff that provided a perfectly suitable Trireme-sized parking spot. We huddled on the bridge to figure out our next move. We definitely needed to see about making repairs as the ship had suffered some damage in the firefight. Lucy was in command.

"Ship, anything on sensors from those Moon Tactical Fighters?"

"No, we appear to have given them the slip, as it were."

"Nice ship. Good ship," Amoz said, as if to a puppy.

If an inter-stellar space ship could wag its tail like a dog, our ship would have. I needed a stiff rye, a nice Earth rye, and bad.

"Guys, not be a downer, I mean I can initiate the needed diagnostic repairs, but I will need a body to remove and replace damaged systems and aid in repairs, you know, like a human body."

"You're so needy ship."

"Shut up Molloy," a surprising number of my colleagues said at once.

"I'm sorry guys, really I am. The repair-bot that originally came with the ship disappeared a few cycles ago," continued the ship.

"That sucks Ship."

"Disappeared?"

"He wasn't being very nice to me and then well, he just upped and disappeared one day."

We all felt a little uneasy at this and exchanged a few glances. We quickly moved on. Maybe it was the slightly sinister note that crept into the otherwise annoyingly upbeat computer voice. I wondered if Space ships saw psychiatrists, before being distracted by the mission at hand.

"Ship how long for the repairs?" asked Manuel.

"I estimate having the ship operational in ninety-four Earth hours."

"So, who stays and helps repair the ship and who goes on the exciting, dangerous mission?" asked Amoz.

"Well, obviously I am going. I need to see this through. Besides, I'm the only one who knows what that Krell-bag Thrown looks like."

"And I'm too good looking not to be seen in public," I said, as Manuel rolled his eyes. "To be serious, it's my case, so I go. Plain and simple."

"Agreed," said Lucy, followed by Manuel.

"That leaves Manuel or Amoz, and we know what Amoz is good for, that is, simply put, goonery," said I.

"Boody, for serious. I have other skills. I do magic tricks, and sometimes juggle, though juggling is hard."

"Well, then Amoz, that decides it," said Manuel sarcastically.

"Yeah, those sledgehammer hands are custom built for things other than juggling delicate little balls," I said.

"There's a sex joke in there somewhere, but we don't have the time," added Lucy.

"Let me finish Boodies. I am okay helping to fix machines. Electrical repair was my minor in college."

"Let me guess what your major was..."

"I only majored in goonery slash thuggery as that's what Poppa always wanted."

"The father that wanted his son to follow in his footsteps,

the age old story."

"Thanks for that Manuel," I said with unbridled sarcasm. "Amoz you continue to surprise. Okay, it's settled, Amoz will stay and help repair Ship. Is Amoz a good enough human body for you Ship?"

"Amoz will do nicely Mister Molloy."

"Molloy, just Molloy, okay Ship?"

"Okay!" said Ship so enthusiastically it caused me to grit my teeth.

"My pops was a legend in goon circles, before he retired. A real legend," Amoz said, lost in thought.

"So it's agreed," said Lucy. "Next topic on the agenda."

The ship seemed to have taken quite a liking to Amoz so everyone was happy. Besides having a seven-foot, three-hundred pound muscle-bound goon with us when trying to subtly procure information on the whereabouts of Thrown was not exactly discreet and what we required was some serious discreeting. Also I wanted Manuel along. He could sneak into most places, scale most walls, crack the best security grids, and make the most devastatingly cutting comments of any of us, bar none. In short, we needed his skill set for this case more than ever.

Next topic on the agenda was the weapons situation and it was not a happy one, as in we hardly had any weapons at all. In fact, we had just two, those being mine and Manuel's, and they were almost out of charge. It was Manuel who came up with the brilliant and unorthodox solution of asking the ship.

"Hey Ship, you have any personnel hand weapons?" he asked.

"As a matter of fact, I do. I had to confiscate them from my last owners. They weren't nice to me like you guys. That's when me and the maintenance-bot were still friends."

Lucy, Manuel and I shared a second uncomfortable look. I wondered what exactly had happened to the ship's last owners. But then I decided the answer to this might cause us all undo stress. Instead I asked the ship if it had any booze hoping lightning might strike twice in the form of positive responses, but was tragically and sadly disappointed.

Ship directed us to the storage compartments were there were four laser rifles and six hand-blasters, all fully charged and ready to fire; quite a nice little score. They were top of the line models too, Excelsior class, and even had intensity settings from stun to four. Amoz took a rifle and a hand-blaster to help guard Ship against any unwelcome visitors, while Manuel. Lucy and I each took a blaster.

The final cog in the plan was land transport and in this too the ship was helpful. Turns out the ship came stocked with a small land skiff, basically a floating platform you could drive. The ship was being extraordinarily helpful actually, and a little voice in my head worried about what dear old St. Murphy would say.

We said our farewells to Amoz and the ship and prepared to leave. I clasped Amoz on the shoulder.

"Be careful Amoz. We'll be back as soon as we can."

"Don't have too much fun without me boodo."

"I promise we'll call the minute things get, uhmmm, interesting."

We departed on the skiff, Manuel driving. It was quite fast and I had to hold onto my hat as Manuel skimmed low, just above the ground. I gave a parting look back at the ship.

"It really is a good thing the ship looks like such a piece of crap. No one will try and steal it if they even find it. I do wonder what happened to its maintenance bot and last crew though."

No one responded to that as the skiff tore across the desert landscape, towards the settlement, a large dust plume billowing behind us. We thought about it in silence though, or at least I did.

<->

WE arrived on the settlement's outskirts without further mishap, although Manuel and Lucy did get into an argument about her original justification for those space tights. I didn't get involved. Manuel sent the skiff on auto-nav back to the ship, as this wasn't the nicest of neighbourhoods to park. Lucy had a com device and could contact the ship for it when we were ready.

I figured the best spot to glean some information was the seediest bar I could find, or the nearest one. Fortunately for us all the bars on Memnon settlement were exceptionally seedy. I wasn't too choosy either, as I needed a good stiff drink about as bad as an extra enthusiastic teetotaller did not.

"Hey barkeep, you got any Earth booze? Earth rye to be specific?"

"He grunted and made over with a bottle of Old Babylon, perhaps the best of the cheap variety and an old stand-by of mine. While he was pouring me a drink Manuel and Lucy fanned out, searching for possible sources of information. A part of me was craving a little nip of that Spider-venom, but sadly the bartender didn't know what the hell I was talking about. This was likely a very good thing.

The bar wasn't overly busy. There were a few regulars in the back playing cards and a few patrons scattered around at various tables. It was quiet and I have always liked quiet bars. However, there was an electric under-current of danger to the place as well. None of the patrons were laughing. They all looked tough. Lucy was all ready attracting some lug-head interest. As was Manuel. I decided to sip my drink in peace and let them each work their charms. That was when a little runt of a man, swarthy, dark hair parted town the middle, and with the narrowest margin of a moustache, sat next to me at the bar. His eyes slightly bulged from his head and he was thin to the point of starvation; what they used to call New York thin.

"You're new here. Might I be of help? My services as guide and companion are available, at very reasonable rates."

"I'm sure they are pal, but listen, I ain't interested."

"But wait, hear me out. For the small price of one drink I will..."

I zoned the little fellow out and focused on the back, where it seemed Manuel and Lucy were in direct competition with one another to see who was best at seducing dead-beat bar flies and/or killers. I watched as Lucy stuck her tongue out at Manuel, and leaned back on a very piratical looking fellow's lap while she stroked his beard and he emitted what possibly could be purring sounds.

"Lazslo Loewenstein, at your service. Now I can introduce..."

"If you don't beat it chum I am going to introduce this bar stool to your small intestine."

The bartender approached and re-filled my glass, shooed the pesky little man away.

"So, what's the deal with Memnon?"

"You know, there's an awful lot of warehouses here. I know that much."

"Thank you, that's very helpful. I mean, who's the players? Ever hear of a human goes by Cal-Ray Thrown?"

"Listen pal, let me give you some free advice. Just drink your drink, avoid making eye contact and most importantly, avoid asking too many questions. You might live longer." He looked me over dubiously. "Maybe."

"I'll keep that in mind."

"Besides I don't like that trench coat. Means trouble."

"Again, I'll keep that in mind. Now, if you'll excuse me I think I see someone I know. There's a robot with one arm over there I think I am acquainted with"

I took my drink over to a dark corner where a matte grey-black, metallic robot body was barely discernible through the gloom. It was a familiar looking robot, and was missing an arm.

"Well, well. Fancy running into you here."

"Hello Molloy."

"I see you made it off the Antipoinnes. What brings you to this rock?"

"Most of me did." The robot looked coldly to its missing arm. "Trying to find work. This seemed like a good a planetoid as any. I need a new arm. You?"

"We're laying low for awhile. Strange coincidence seeing you here."

"Strange indeed Molloy," the robot said in a more sinister manner than usual, which was quite a difficult feat. The robot stared at me with the same cold look and then winked.

Just then the bartender brought a baseball bat down onto the table gathering everyone's attention. Though baseball is a long extinct sport, the baseball bat has lived on, as almost a ceremonial piece in every bartender's repertoire, or uniform, kind of like my trench coat and fedora.

"I just got a call. Memnon P.D. are on their way to this district in force. The bar is closed. Get out."

The bartender was greeted by muted stares, and a lot of furtive glances towards the back. The bartender slammed the baseball bat on the bar once more. Everyone winced and was moved to action, except the robot.

"Memnon P.D. are looking for someone. They'll be rounding up the usual suspects. Get out of my bar. We're closed. I want no trouble and no coppers here."

At this the whole bar, en masse, disappeared out the back exit. Lucy was unceremoniously tossed from the lap she was lounging upon, as was Manuel. No one in the bar, it seemed, like to deal with Memnon P.D. We huddled up and quickly decided it would be best to follow everyone out back. I looked over for the one-armed robot, but he was gone.

The bar exited into an alley. By the time we got there the other patrons had mostly vanished into the surroundings and it was pretty much deserted. It was dark and dusty and smelled like death, like most alleys I was familiar with. At the sound of sirens we took off in the only direction that seemed away from them, heading deeper into the settlement.

Five minutes and several twists and turns later we entered a courtyard and were beginning to think we'd given Memnon P.D. the slip. Certainly the sounds of police sirens had all but disappeared into the background. We gazed about and pondered our next move. I personally thought hitting another bar a fantastic idea when suddenly the whole place was lit up with laser blasts and we had to scramble for cover. It was a good thing that whoever was shooting was not that great of a shot as no one was hit. But we were effectively pinned down behind a low wall at the back of the courtyard and the barrage was intense. I looked behind us and there was no back exit or alley, nothing but a thirty foot high cement wall, which was becoming increasingly peppered with laser burn marks. Things were not looking good. While at the courtyard entrance black and silver uniformed men with laser rifles jogged around, occasionally shooting in our general direction, occasionally bumping into one another. They all wore large opaque bubble-shaped helmets fitted with the narrowest of eye slots and puffy silver moon boots. They all were going 'hup-hup-hup' and bouncing up and down, like they were boxers or in some kind of boot camp. This along with those moon boots, was profoundly annoying, at least to Manuel and I, as we both returned fire and they scampered behind some generators and machinery for cover. (*I later found out these were Memnon Vice cops and the reason for the narrow eye slits was that their visibility is purposely obscured so they don't get corrupted by all the vice around them.*)

I stood up to get a better view and dust myself off when Lucy grabbed me violently by the arm.

"Get down," she screamed and pulled me down just as the metal bin directly behind where I was standing was peppered with laser blasts. ""Be careful Molloy!"

"I didn't know you cared."

She made a face and didn't further respond so I just took a deep breath and stayed low. We, in fact, hunkered down as if our lives depended on it, which of course, they did. After a few minutes of indiscriminate laser fire there was a calming down period followed by a general detente. One of them, their spokesmen or leader, brought out a sleek megaphone, which was also black and matched his uniform quite nicely.

"Stop Earth humans, or we'll shoot."

"You all ready shot!" I shouted back.

"What's that?"

"I said you all ready shot."

"Oh, right. That was Johnson. He's new."

"Sorry, my bad," one of the cops shouted, presumably Johnson.

"It was everyone shooting, you jveks!" shouted Lucy.

Lucy had a thing with pointing out people's flaws and inaccuracies. It made her not so popular at dinner parties. The Memnon police paused to confer with one another. We could see the tops of their bubble helmets huddled in conference. Unfortunately they had us pinned down and all avenues of escape were cut off. They broke up their little huddle with a series of high fives. The one with the megaphone broke off from the rest and faced us from behind the now smoking generator.

"You have a point. We did all ready shoot," he said.

"Thank you." shouted Lucy.

"Well, you know, we're not unreasonable."

"Ahhhm okay," shouted Lucy. "So, now what?"

"Well, now is usually the point where you offer us a bribe."

"A nice bribe. Something pretty," another space cop said.

"Shhhh! Let me deal with them. I have the megaphone. When you have the megaphone you can talk to them."

"But Grant, you always have the megaphone..."

"Shut up Lamar!"

While they argued amongst themselves, Lucy turned to Manuel and I: "They must be Memnon Vice. I've heard they're super corrupt."

"That sort of makes sense, I guess," said Manuel.

The one with the megaphone was back: "Yoo-hoo, any thoughts on that last bit, or you know..."

He then signalled to his comrades and another barrage of laser fire peppered our position. We huddled tight in whispered discussion.

"They aren't too subtle are they," I said. "What we need is some credits or something to offer as a bribe."

"We are out of credits and don't have anything though."

"Manuel could offer them some fashion advice."

"I don't think they'd appreciate that," said Lucy. "Wait a second."

The laser barrage had again fallen off. It seemed they set their rifles on low, my theory being that if you kill or vaporize your quarry you couldn't really then expect them to pay you a bribe. That and they missed a lot and insurance rates would be through the roof if they kept blowing holes and/or disintegrating things. We turned our blasters down too, to stun even, it being decided that space cop killer was something none of us wanted on our curriculum vitae. Lucy peaked her head over the wall and surveyed the scene.

"Hey, we would like to help, but you see, we're a little short this month. We don't have any credits or money. Would you take fashion advice? Or a bribe, on credit?"

Another serious and prolonged laser barrage. Then the M.P.D. huddled up again, presumably in conference.

"I guess they are a little touchy re: fashion tips or graft on credit," I said.

"Probably mostly the credit part," added Manuel.

The megaphone issued a blast of feedback equally scaring us and the man holding it. He turned it down looking a bit flustered.

"No, we don't take bribes on credit. I guess we'll just have to do things the old fashioned way then," he said cheerfully.

He gestured to a colleague: "Hey Joey, go get the frag launcher."

He realized he was still speaking into the megaphone and quickly set it down looking even more embarrassed. Joey disappeared.

"Oh dear, They could launch a fragger grenade over the wall and that will be that."

"Oh dear is right."

"Hey wait a second guys." Lucy shouted at our persecutors. "Give us a second, will you?"

"Okay, hold on. I think we'll let you go now. No need to worry," said the megaphone.

But we could see Joey was back, and with a shoulder-firing frag II class grenade launcher, no less. He was clearly bluffing about letting us go to buy time for Joey, which was not very sporting of him, I had to say.

"Lucy, call Amoz on the com. Seems we need a rescue," I said.

"Oh right, the com!" she replied.

She un-clipped the little com device from her waist and tapped it several times, but it wasn't functioning.

"I can't get a signal pinned down here like this."

"Frekking typical!" said I.

"It's no good. I have to get up there on the wall."

"Lucy, be careful," said Manuel.

She climbed on top of the wall and smiled at us: "They wouldn't shoot a lady in space tights, would they?"

"This is your last chance to surrender. We'll give you a count of ten," said the megaphone speaker.

"Amoz, come in. We need help..."

"One... two..."

"We're pinned down. Amoz, do you copy?"

"...three. Fire!"

We watched in horror as Joey launched the frag grenade. It sailed through the air in an upward arc. Manuel and I huddled against the base of the wall and watched as it detonated right above where Lucy was still trying to get a call in to Amoz. We were showered in dust and dirt and grenade fragments. Half the wall little wall we sheltered behind had come down. When the dust cleared I saw Manuel was miraculously unhurt minus a few scratches and cuts. My head was pounding and there was blood in my eyes. Also my side was screaming in pain, but I didn't care. There in a pile of rocks and shrapnel, covered in dust and mortar and bricks, was Lucy, unmoving.

"Lucy!" I shouted, but my ears were ringing so much I could barely hear myself.

I rushed over to her, expecting the worse. I cleared off the rubble and tried to see if she was okay, but the ringing in my head was disorienting. She didn't move when I touched her.

Manuel was up and shouting something about that not being ten seconds, and swearing viciously in several languages, his blaster firing again and again. But I was concentrating on her. So brave and reckless and now unmoving. I was cradling Lucy's head which was bleeding from a small gash on her forehead. I used my trench coat as a pillow under her neck, expecting the worst. Shrapnel from the bomb was all around her and embedded in her space tights. I gently brushed at them expecting a flow of blood, but oddly the pieces just fell off, not having pierced through. Impossible, I thought before Manuel shook me violently. Laser blasts now began to impact all around us as the smoke and dust cleared.

"Molloy, we got to go. Get it together, we're in it bad."

"Manuel, it wasn't supposed to go down this way."

"Molloy, we got to go!" he shouted.

That was when she breathed and moaned and turned on her shoulder. Lucy was alive. I cradled her to my chest and wanted to cry tears of release and joy, but we were rather busy. They continued to shoot at us. Manuel returned fire, his blaster blazing.

"Lucy you're all right. I was worried there for a second."

"I don't just wear these to look good, sailor. That's Seralian weave. Best armour in the three systems." She coughed, looked at me weakly and smiled. "Still though. Ow."

"Come on."

I rose, carrying her in my arms, leaving the trench coat where it lay in the dust and rubble. My side ached horribly and felt slippery and wet. We needed an exit and fast. That was when from behind a figure moved towards us out of the smoke. I wheeled and braced to fire.

"Molloy, don't shoot. It's Lazslo. Come with me. I can get you all out of here. Quickly before the dust settles and they come."

<->

IT turned out there was a secret passageway hidden in the wall behind us. Lazslo, the annoying fellow from the bar, had come to rescue us, which considerably increased my opinion of him almost instantly.

After closing the hidden entrance behind he led us dazed and dirtied into a labyrinth of tunnels. Apparently these were used by the criminal element for smuggling and evading the M.P.D. and interconnected much of the settlement. I was weak and wearied and Lucy kept falling in and out of consciousness. Manuel was in not much better shape than I, but between us we managed to support Lucy and drag her along. So it was with relief when Lazslo eventually led us to an empty warehouse type room.

When Manuel commented about the state of my shoes it lacked his usual bite and wit. He'd noticed they were covered in blood as was much of my trouser leg. I muttered something about another large dry cleaning bill before collapsing to the floor.

I woke up on an old military-style cot. Manuel was busy with thread between his teeth and a needle in hand. He was sewing. He gave me some kind of moon whisky and it was good. I knew this was moon whisky as it had a picture of a moon on the bottle and was labelled 'Memnon's Finest'. It felt like I'd all ready had quite a bit of it. I was feeling no pain at any rate and my vision was cloudier than a muddied lake.

"Manuel, why are you hovering over me? And if my trousers are ripped, at least let me take them off before you try and mend them."

"Hush Molloy. You've lost some blood," said Lucy kindly, her face materializing above me.

"You should've said you'd got hit," said Manuel somewhat angrily. "Not sewing your slacks, Molloy."

He grabbed the bottle.

"Hey, I was using that..."

But that was all I could get out as he proceeded to pour it over his true target of tailoring, namely my freshly sewed up side. I shouted something very loudly that was quite definitely unprintable. And then everything went black.

I came to sometime the next morning. I could tell because the light coming through cracks in the high window felt like icepicks entering my brain. This thanks to that old Memnon's

Finest, no doubt. The bottle was empty except for one swig, sitting beside the cot. I dutifully emptied it. Manuel had done a fine job patching me up. The bleeding had stopped and there was a first class sticky bandage covering his stitches. It hurt though. The good thing was it was now more of a dull throb, down from a screaming roar, which was progress. It turned out Lucy, due to her fancy Seralian weave space tights-bodysuit, was the least injured of all three of us. She and Manuel were seated on crates, munching some ration biscuits. Lazslo was no where to be seen.

I slowly got up and joined them. Manuel shoved a plate of biscuits and a tin cup of water at me. He was still mad I'd gone and gotten myself hurt. It was a touching kind of mad. And I gripped his shoulder in a mute thank you for all he'd done for me. He shrugged and walked off. This was basically how our relationship worked and how we showed each other we cared.

"Where's Lazslo? Out selling us out to the highest bidder?"

"Actually, just you. While you were unconscious Manuel and I switched sides. We're selling you out."

"Very funny Lucy."

"Lazslo went to get supplies and see what the heat is like."

"You trust him?"

"Not sure yet. He seems okay. You better eat. He's a little slippery, but I think it's just surface slippery."

"Like a fish."

"I am not sure I get you."

"Some fish exude a mucous like substance that covers their scales."

"Sure Molloy. Eat some food. You need your strength back."

I ate and mused on fish scale mucous to take my mind off the taste of the biscuits, which were unbreakable by human standards. And I almost broke a tooth. Manuel came back and showed me the trick of dipping them in water first, which made them almost edible. I forced down two and drank a lot of water.

It appeared that in the chaos of the fight Lucy had lost the communicator, so reaching the ship for help was not on the menu. We were, for the time being, on our own. I was pretty sure that com device would have tasted better than the biscuits, speaking of menus. Also lost was my trusty trench coat. But everyone agreed the trench coat was way too conspicuous anyways and it was best left behind. I had to grudgingly agree to this logic, although technically I could lose my detective ticket for not operating in uniform if ever anyone decided on a formal complaint to D.I.C.K. headquarters in Tex-Arkana, back on Earth. But we had a lot more serious things to worry about then losing my license at the moment.

(*D.I.C.K. is an acronym for Detectives, Investigators, Criminologists and Killjoys, respectively, for all you jveck-heads who've been wondering all this time.*)

Lazslo returned with some provisions and news that the heat from M.P.D. Vice had died down. Apparently they were all ready happily extorting bribes from other newcomers to the moon. It was a good thing we hadn't iced any of them. That's the kind of heat that never dies down. Lazslo's eel-like presence was gaining more charm. But I was always suspicious of anyone wanting to help me, as a rule.

"How come you helped us anyways? What's in it for you?"

"Lay off him Molloy. He did just save us."

"Everyone has an angle. I want to know his," I replied just as Lazslo passed within earshot.

"I saved you, Molloy, because when I overheard you at the bar I realized that both of our goals may overlap."

"What do you mean Lazslo?"

"Cal Ray Thrown," Lazslo hissed.

It turned out Lazslo was acquainted with Cal Ray and they were not on the best of terms. He told us about Thrown, how he was a collector of sorts and a fence and a 'notorious utter bastard'.

"That's good," I said. "I always feel better stealing from utter bastards."

Apparently Thrown had quite the reputation on Memnon. And when Lazslo had a deal go sour Thrown took his only daughter for collateral on the debt and she'd been not heard from since. Lazslo desperately wanted to rescue his daughter, but he needed help once inside and a distraction while he busted her loose. We told him we wanted also to break in, although our exact target we didn't entrust him with. He told us a little about the compound, how it was surrounded with a high, spiked wall patrolled by guards and other security apparatus. Lazslo said he knew a way to get us in, if we in turn helped him with his rescue or at least distracted security from him while he carried it out.

"So, you see," stated Lazslo, "I need to get inside his compound as much or more as you do."

"Okay Lazslo, you've got a deal."

"I get you in. You distract or occupy the security. There we part ways. I go after my goal, you your own. That is the deal."

"As long as you can get us in undetected you have a deal Lazslo," said Lucy, and they shook on it.

Who knew if Lazslo was being honest about his daughter. He wanted something from inside and so did we. That was all that mattered. Like I said earlier, why ask questions you might not like the answers too. Besides if he betrayed us we had him outgunned. And if he betrayed us, we all agreed, our blasters would certainly not be set on stun.

We waited another twenty-four Earth hours before we got under way. Though the clock was ticking we needed time to study the situation and come up with a better plan other than breaking in and running around looking in every closet, which was just about what the former plan had been. Also, Manuel thought I needed time to let my stitches set, and he was like a mother Grizzly bear in this matter and not to be trifled with. So we spent the day getting as much info about the compound as we could from Lazslo. We also debated contacting Ship and Amoz, but the idea of exposing ourselves and using an open, public com where anyone could be listening was decided to be a bad idea. We couldn't risk the ship being discovered as we would be needing a way off this rock, if we survived and managed to escape. So, we were on our own.

The plan was to make our move to coincide with the changing of the guard, which, according to Lazslo, took place at 15 o'clock Memnon time, every afternoon. Lazslo would get us inside and then we would either find the object or find Thrown and force him to tell us where it is. It wasn't much of a better plan than we originally had, but now at least we new a basic layout of the compound, and also confirmation that Thrown was an utter bastard, which would help, in case we had to get rough.

And so we headed back into the tunnels, led by Lazslo, after an incredibly unsatisfying lunch of the iron-hard biscuits and water. My side was aching, but at least my inside's were staying where they were supposed to. We were all dressed in the same black, tight fitting clothes provided by Lazslo. Lucy had her famous space-tights/bodysuit on underneath. In the shadows of the tunnels we were almost invisible. If we were discovered we were to say we were freelance mimes on our way to a performance, except seeing as mimes don't talk, we would have to mime this, and hope for better lighting before they started shooting.

I walked with Manuel in the rear, feeling naked without my trench coat and not a little chilled, despite the turtle-neck sweater. Lazslo led, with Lucy walking tightly behind him, blaster in her hand. She looked beautiful. And deadly. My kinda gal. We encountered no enemies, nor anyone; not even an insurance salesperson. It was, in fact, quite a nice walk. I silently wondered how Ship and Amoz were doing.

After an hour or so Lazslo gestured us in to a huddle in a completely un-interesting and nondescript portion of tunnel.

"We have arrived. Are you ready? On the other side of this wall lies the underbelly of the secured compound of Cal-Ray Thrown, the biggest krellbag in the three systems."

We nodded and checked our blasters. Lazslo felt along the stone wall, as if seeking something.

"These tunnels have been here for decades, long before Thrown. Let's hope he doesn't know all of their secrets," he continued.

Lazslo grunted in triumph, pushed in a panel and a hidden door swung open. Inside the door was another tunnel, exactly the same as the one we'd left.

"Above us will be Thrown's men. Be on your guard."

Inside was wetter than I expected, and more humid. The walls were dank and dripping. Lazslo was scouting up a head. Lucy, Manuel and I were a little more cautious, walking together. One thing was one my mind. And that was the Famous Jewelled Phallus of Arkon III the Credulous, and the fact I knew so little about it.

"Lucy, tell us what were looking for. What does the incredible Phallus of Arkon III look like?"

"Yes, Lucy, you have been rather vague on that," added Manuel.

"Oh, it's fabulous and bejewelled, you know. And like really, really valuable. It's just so really nice. One of the nicest things ever..."

"Yeah, but what does it actually look like?" asked Manuel. "I mean, we need to know to find it, right?"

"Well, I'm pretty sure it's phallus shaped."

"Pretty sure. Wait, what?"

"You mean you've never seen it?" I said, a little flabbergasted.

"Not as such, no."

"I thought you said it was stolen from you?"

"It was. It was stolen before I got to look at it though. Like, in transit."

"Well, how do we know what it'll look like?" said an exasperated Manuel. "My shoes are getting wrecked down here Lucy!"

"We'll know it when we see it. It's really, really... nice. It'll be in his vault or on display with fancy lighting and bells and things."

"I just new it wouldn't be easy," I said to no one in general. "Why is it never easy?"

I crossed my fingers and said a small prayer to Saint Murphy. Lazslo was getting quite a bit ahead of us I noticed.

And my side was itching.

"We could have solved the ketchup package case and be rich by now Molloy. But no, you have to go traipsing across the three systems on a fool's errand for a priceless artifact we don't even know what it looks like?" whispered Manuel ferociously, before suddenly sneezing three times in rapid succession.

All three of us froze. Lucy and I looked at one another and said in unison: "Danger!"

That was when Lazslo, already twenty feet ahead, took off running and did not look back. Suddenly three guards emerged from the shadows and surrounded us, weapons drawn. We didn't have a chance. There being no other course of action to take we raised our hands. I shrugged and smiled at the guard closest to me.

"Would you believe we're freelance mimes who've took on wrong turn on our way to a street art performance?"

"If you were mimes, where are your berets?" said at guard, sneering.

"Yeah, mimes gots berets, and make-up," mentioned another guard as he roughly searched and disarmed us. "Nice turtlenecks though."

"Thanks."

It was too late to play mute and do the mime routine. I'd blown it. Back in the shadows, behind the third guard, I saw movement, and wondered if I was finally going to meet the famous Cal-Ray Thrown. Disconcertingly, and also from the shadows, a laser rifle could be heard powering up.

"They are not mimes, you fools," issued a familiar, metallic voice.

Out of the darkness stepped my old acquaintance. He was holding a heavy laser rifle effortlessly with his one robot arm.

"Hello again Molloy."

"I knew it was too big a coincidence seeing your here."

"The Makotai want that ship back. Apparently it was very naughty and lied about some of its features at its last diagnostic. It's supposed to have built in honesty protocols... But you just can't trust machines these days."

"You can say that again," said I.

"Sorry Molloy, business is business. You just bought me a new arm."

"You're working for the Makotai?"

"And Thrown. Which is great. Double dipping, which is the best kind of dipping. See, for now I hand you over to Thrown, and let you rot in his prison until the two weeks expire on the Makotai bounty. Then I kill you all, and legally collect it when I bring them your corpses. Win-win."

"Well, except for us."

"Yes, except for you all. You all lose."

The robot levelled the rifle at us and the guards hurriedly backed off. "Or I could just kill you now, and take your ship for myself."

"No, no, we like the first plan."

"Prison sounds nice. We could use some time off."

"Throw them in manacles. And find the other one," said the robot to the guards.

I would have asked the robot's name, but we had all ready been through so much I thought it might be awkward, and he might therefore get offended, and then me might just shoot us all. So I kept mute.

One of the guards went off, presumably searching for Lazslo, and the others led us away in manacles they had brought for just such an occasion.

"Sheesh, Lucy is there anything else you want to share? Anything you haven't been forthright about?"

"Yes."

"Oh dear."

"No talking," said one of the guards and slammed the butt of his gun into my lower back.

I buckled over and went down hard, grimacing in pain, trying not to cry out, but not succeeding very well. One of the guards roughly dragged me to my feet.

"Well, Lucy?"

"This isn't my natural hair colour."

"But you have met this Thrown?" asked Manuel.

"Oh yes. He knows me all too well. You'll see when he greets us," said Lucy.

"I said no talking," the other guard barked at me.

"I heard you the first time," I said, getting annoyed.

This time the rifle butt connected with my forehead and I was down and out. But the joke was on them, because now they had to carry and/or drag me all the way to the cells.

# CHAPTER EIGHT

# CHAPTER EIGHT

THE NEXT THING I knew I awoke in chains in one of Thrown's prison cells. My head was pounding and my side ached. I took a moment to take things in. It was a typical prison with cells with metal bars and cement walls and floors. I wondered if they imported the straw that covered the floors. There wasn't any vegetation on Memnon, as far as I could tell. Either way, it was a nice touch; very retro.

Lucy and Manuel were standing in the corner, staring at another cell. They seemed to be doing just fine. I made a couple well timed grunts in order to get their attention before bursting into a fit of ill-timed coughing. I needed a strong drink is what I needed.

"Ugh. Anyone have any spider-cide?"

"Molloy's awake, and he's babbling," said Manuel.

They wandered over to me.

"Molloy, you sure get hit a lot, huh?" said Lucy, not unkindly.

I did not dignify that with an answer. She then brought a tin up she filled with water from a barrel, that I hoped did not double as the cell privy.

"Hey, how come you guys are sans les manacles?"

"They don't seem to like you as much as us Molloy. This seems to be a pretty consistent reaction to most people we meet. Is it always this way Manuel?"

"Always," replied Manuel.

I doubly didn't dignify that with an answer and tried some water. I felt a great deal better almost immediately.

"Manuel and I have been figuring out what to do," she said. "And?"

"We looked at things from every angle and have decided that from every angle we are equally screwed."

"As long as you've done the mathematics Lucy."

I took another long sip of water, laid back down on the cot and closed my eyes. As this did not have the desired effect I decided to get up and walk around to clear my head. I moved to our one small, barred window and looked out onto a courtyard far below. I reflected on why things always seemed to work out the way they did for me, figuring that there must be several hundred people with Molloy shaped voodoo dolls out there with way too much time on their hands.

There were men down there in the courtyard, busy as space bees, setting up three poles each with red targets painted on them, perfect for a firing squad, I'd imagine. Not a bad way to go out. I wondered if they give you a last glass of rye before they shot you.

I was was jolted from this charming reverie by the clanging of steel doors. All three of us approached the front bars expecting any number of unpleasant things from interrogators to torturers, or perhaps just Thrown, come to gloat, and then interrogate and torture us. But it was none of those things. In fact, it was just breakfast, served by a puttering servant-bot that had seen better days. And it was not a bad breakfast at all, considering.

It certainly smelled okay, and was hot. Both Manuel and I waited expectantly as Lucy dug into her tray with an appetite. After a few seconds she was still busily eating, and not convulsing on the floor in a foetal position, so we ripped the covers off our own trays and dug in. The food, which consisted of green nutrient paste on cardboard-like crackers and some form of watery tea, was like a gourmet meal compared to the meagre, bullet-hard ration biscuits of the last few days. The robot waited patiently outside the bars and seemed embarrassed for us.

This robot didn't have any language circuits, just an assortment of beeps, or was maybe just a snob, I couldn't tell. Having finished disapproving of us it moved to the adjacent cell and prodded a heap of blankets with a pole which extended from a small port on its side. This elicited a groan and I realized for the first time we were not the sole occupants of these cells. With a curse a tin mug was flung from the shadows, hitting the robot and causing it to beep ferociously before wheeling out of the room in what could only be called a huff.

What stirred in the corner of the adjacent cell uttered another groan and then a hand covered in dried blood reached out and grabbed the food tray the robot had left and swept it inside the cell.

I moved to get a better view and was surprised to see none other than Lazslo Loewenstein crouched low and eating with his fingers. He was bloodied, swollen and bandaged. It seemed like they'd worked him over a lot.

"Well, I guess that solves the riddle of whether or not the little bastard betrayed us," I said.

"They brought him in a few hours ago. Looks like the did a lot of work on him," said Manuel. "He's a tough little mug, I'll give him that. Isn't that right Lazslo?" I said.

Lazslo grunted and with some effort rose and moved to the front of his cell where he propped himself on the bars to keep upright. He looked in rough shape. One of his eyes was swollen shut.

"I didn't tell them no things," he said, with a lisp. "I only want to find my daughter. If you were not so incompetent as to get caught right away I would've had a chance."

"Lazslo, they were on us the minute we entered the compound. We didn't stand a chance," said Lucy.

Lazslo grunted and ate some more paste. He looked barely alive, pale and ghoulish. He smiled at us and it made him look even worse.

"They must've been aware of the secret passageway all

along. My sources were apparently in error on this. You were supposed to be a more talented distraction though," he said.

"So you used us Lazslo," I said.

"I used you. You used me. That's how business works on Memnon."

It was how business worked everywhere in the three systems. I couldn't really hold a grudge. It was how the systems worked. And I was pretty impressed he took such a beating and was still defiant. Whether he actually talked or not was anyone's guess. Lazslo moved to the back of his cell, and looked out his window, which was similar to ours.

"Oh well. Better luck next time," he mused philosophically.

"Better luck next time! There won't be a next time you runting kveck! We're stuck in a dungeon and likely to face a firing squad any minute for all we know?" I shouted, losing my cool.

"Look on the bright side Molloy," said Lazlso. "At least there's a nice view."

"It's a view of the execution ground you dolt!"

"You're too negative Molloy. You're not dead yet. You need to relax a little."

I moved to the corner farthest from the little runt's cell. I sat down and finished my meal. Relax a little, he says.

<->

IT was another three days before there was another commotion of any interest, aside from being fed the paste and crackers by the tottering robot, which had become the highlight of each day. Time was ticking and we had no plan of what to do or how to escape. Each day the execution ground in the square below, if that's what it really was, got a little more complete. There were now benches, and stanchions with velvet rope. Today they put up bunting, and not just any old bunting: really nice bunting. Manuel was becoming increasingly agitated and worried as that bunting, he said, clashed heavily with our outfits, and he just didn't want to die that way. When I posited the theory that nothing clashed with black I received a snarled response that was as scathing as it was unprintable. Meanwhile, I was still in shackles and thought it really unfair that nobody else was, or had been, for days. I politely asked the robot to bring some for everyone else, but it just beeped at me in response, like a total jerk.

However, on the third day came the commotion we'd been waiting for and/or dreading. Lucy was clearly in the dreading camp. She had barely eaten any of her paste the last two days.

After the prerequisite banging and clanging of iron doors a grand procession entered our prison chamber. Well, two guards, my favourite one-armed robot, and finally, a small, rotund, balding little man.

"None other than Cal-Ray Thrown himself," said Lucy.

He approached our cell slowly and inspected us as one might pickled eggs in a not very clean jar. He smiled and it was a pleasant kind smile. His eyes, however, were ice cold. His comb-over was immaculate.

"Hello Lucy. You have a lot of nerve coming here. After what you tried last time," said Thrown.

"Baby, that was all a misunderstanding. I've come to apologize."

"Baby?" Manuel and I gasped simultaneously.

Thrown ignored us, intent on Lucy.

"I like the turtle-neck. It's a nice look for you."

"Why thank you," said Manuel, dryly.

"I was talking to the lady. But very amusing," said Thrown.

He looked over to the cell in which the slumped and damaged form of Lazslo lay. And again he smiled that big, happy smile.

"We tortured your little friend. I suggest you find better company than the lowliest scum on Memnon. Apparently he is under the notion his daughter is a prisoner here. But I am afraid you four are the only guests, as you can see. I suppose she could be on staff, maybe one of our sex slaves, eh little friend? Maybe I will use her badly tonight."

Like a cat Lazslo leapt to his feet, approached the bars of

his cell.

"You jvecking grand douche-hole."

Thrown gesture to the one-armed robot who now stepped forward, raised a small device and sent blue tongues of electricity into the cell. Lazslo convulsed in agony as the electrical fire crawled all over him. He collapsed to the floor, twitching uncontrollably.

"Enough robot. Just hurt him. Don't kill him. Yet." He turned back to our cell. "My this is fun. So thankful you fellows decided to drop in. Things were getting a little boring around here."

His eyes were cold, but the smile was consistently there. It was unsettling. He turned back to Lucy and sighed.

"Lucy, you really should not have come back. I can't forgive what you tried to do. You must know that."

"Leave Lucy alone. It was all our plan. We strong-armed her into it," I stated, surprising even myself.

"You stole it from her in the first place!" added Manuel, after giving me a seriously questioning look.

"Is that what she told you? Well, she lied? We were partners. We were more than partners, we were lovers. Oh yes. And once she found out about the object, she tried to betray me. She crashed my favourite space ship. My lucky favourite space ship."

"Was that when we came in?" I asked Lucy, under my breath.

"No, this was a different ship."

"You sure crash a lot of spaceships, huh?"

"It gets you noticed."

"I'll say."

"Enough! You two, quit whispering! Robot!"

The one-armed robot moved towards me and gave me just the smallest taste of his blue electrical fire, just enough to bring me to my knees. It really, really hurt. My clothes were slightly smouldering. From my knees I looked across and could see Lazslo recovering in the other cell. He had never even let out a scream and had received considerably more than I had endured. He was one tough hombré.

"But I found out her plans, didn't I Lucy," continued Thrown. "And foiled them as easily as I foiled you this time. Pathetic really, you poor saps. You should go to planning school or something. So you can learn how to make better plans."

"So you did obtain the Famous Jewelled Phallus of Arkon III the Credulous?" asked Lucy, in an awed whisper.

"Yes, Lucy, I did, at considerable expense and effort mind you. And it is magnificent!"

"So, it is real after all." I said.

"Of course, it's real. But I have found once I got it," continued Cal-Ray Thrown, "arranging to find a buyer for a legendary, unbreakable adamantine object, carved from unknown alien technology, and the most sought after invaluable item in the three systems, is no easy thing. Who can afford what is priceless? How do you even haggle for it?"

"And everyone, I mean everyone, wants to kill you for it!" chimed in a guard, happily.

"Yes," said Thrown, eyeing the guard suspiciously. "There's that. And then there's also the curse."

"The curse is real too?" Asked Manuel. "Molloy, I swear this was the dumbest case you ever took!"

"Manuel, this is not the time or place for..."

And didn't the robot hit me with another short burst of that blue electric.

"I take that back," Manuel hissed. "All the cases you take end up like this!"

"Why is it only just me you're shocking?" I stammered, getting riled once more. "I mean, everyone is frekking talking!"

And the robot hit me again and longer this time. I fell flat on my face performing a St. Vitus dance for the ages. Every cell in my body hurt. After taking a moment to gather my thoughts and study my options I decided to keep mute for a while. I was really beginning to dislike that robot quite profoundly.

Thrown gave us all an icy glance.

"Anymore interruptions?"

We all kept our mouths shut, though I could tell Lucy wanted to say something.

"Good. At first I scoffed at the idea of the curse. I mean sure, historically, everyone who has publicly possessed the artifact has come to a quick and violent end, but it's a tough galaxy, am I right? I thought it was superstition frankly. And then my couriers who unknowingly had it in their possession all died shortly after I received it. It's been in a closet ever since. I'm afraid even to touch it."

"You haven't even touched it?" said Lucy.

And the robot shocked me again.

"Come on now!" said I.

Manuel came to help me up. The shackles felt three times as heavy as before. He whispered in my ear.

"See Molloy, my plan for looking in closets was a good one!"

Thrown seemed ever so pleased with himself. He nodded to the robot and his guards before turning back to us.

"And now I must go."

"Now wait a second Thrown. You've made a big mistake. Let's talk like civilized men here. We can work something out," I said, and braced for another jolt.

"Work out this, whatever your name is, which I don't care. Tomorrow at dawn we are all going on a little walk down to the courtyard below where there will be a little marksmanship display. Guess who the targets are? There shall be three."

"Looking forward to it Thrown," said Lucy, with obvious fake bravado. "You haven't won yet."

"See you bright in early in the courtyard my dears!" said Thrown, smiling ear to ear.

He exited the room, gesturing first for one of the guards to remain behind.

"Enjoy your stay Molloy and friends," said the robot, and went to leave.

"Wait robot! If we're dead, vaporized, you won't get your double pay day," I said.

The robot paused. "Thrown has promised me your bodies,

Earthman. No one's getting vaporized, just deadorized. And no one will notice if you smell a few days deader or not, so I'll get my bounty. Thanks for caring though."

The one-armed robot laughed and eerie, haunting, artificial intelligence kind of laugh and exited. It made me feel sick to my stomach. The guard who stayed leaned against the wall. He smiled and waved a lot, whenever one of us made eye-contact, which was odd, being as he was fully aware of, and likely taking part in, our execution tomorrow at dawn. I figured he was just a happy person who loved his job. I waved back, but my heart wasn't really in it.

<->

DAWN. The serving-bot brought us the same watery tea and crackers with paste, but none of us really had an appetite. It was all looking rather bleak. A different guard watched over us near the entrance. I sipped my tea and relished it as quite possibly the last liquid I would ever get a chance to imbibe. It wasn't long before two more guards came. They unlocked the door and lead us three out of our cell. They even removed my manacles. Lazslo was left behind. Maybe they were giving him time to heal before they executed him too, I thought, grimly.

Outside in the courtyard was bright. We were each given t-shirts with red and yellow targets printed on them. Manuel was happier as these didn't clash so much with the bunting. I wouldn't say he was ecstatic, as we were about to be executed, but he was definitely happier than before. It annoyed me how the guards hummed a happy tune while they forced each of our backs to a stake and tied our hands behind it. About fifty paces distant were five guards and the one-armed robot, each with his own laser rifle with scope. To their left was a small bar and some lawn chairs where perched Cal-Ray Thrown and several other spectators. They were being served cocktails by a waiter. My salivary glands went into over drive.

But apparently the cocktails were not meant for the main act, namely us, which was further disheartening. Nor were they for the guards, which was kind of reassuring, as there is nothing less classy than a tipsy firing squad. The sun was rising and it was getting hot. The t-shirt over top of the turtle-neck was making me sweat and the wool was getting itchy. I also couldn't scratch the itch on my nose what with being tied hands behind back to the pole.

There was a speech and someone performed a poem, but I wasn't paying much attention. I was staring at those rifles. Then the main event began: us dying. The five guards and one-armed robot all lined up. A much smaller robot then appeared and played a tawdry drum roll recording. All else was silent. Thrown stood up from his lawn-chair; a red straw dangled from his lips.

"Ready..."

The men and robot as one raised their laser rifles to position and took aim. I turned to Manuel who sneezed, appropriately.

"Manuel, it's been a good ride. We had some good times."

"Yes, boss, it has. We did."

"...Aim..."

"Goodbye Lucy."

"Goodbye Molloy."

"Fi..."

Just as Cal-Ray Thrown was about to say 'fire' there was a sharp wind at our backs as something swooped low from behind us. That something was firing directly at the execution squad who scattered like rabbits before a series of laser blasts, all except the robot who stood his ground and started firing back. That something was Amoz on the land skiff. As he leapt off, blazing away, even the robot was forced to halt its attack and seek cover.

"Amoz, I could kiss you!" said I.

"Hello Boodies."

Amoz now quickly untied Lucy, Manuel and I. A blaster was thrust in my hand. Manuel was handed a laser rifle, and Lucy a pistol. In the background Thrown was yelling up a storm and the guards had re-grouped after their initial retreat and started firing back.

"I finished fixing Ship. Just got your distress call," Amoz shouted, above the din, laying down covering fire.

"What? I sent that days ago!" said Lucy, also firing.

"Really? Ship just told me about it a few hours ago. I guess it wanted me to stay and complete repairs."

"That ship is a piece of work," said Manuel.

"You're telling me!" cried Lucy.

Laser blasts were incoming and getting much too close for comfort.

"We need some cover!" shouted Manuel.

I blasted away, aiming for the robot, but missed as he dived, He rolled and fired back, hitting the stake I was sheltering behind, inches from my head.

"Manuel's right! Fall back," I shouted.

We were completely in the open and needed to find cover. But, on the bright side, I was finally able to scratch my nose.

"Amoz get that skiff out of here, before it's damaged. We'll need it to get away," Lucy shouted.

"We aren't leaving?" I said.

Both sides were firing and withdrawing, as there was no cover in the square for anyone. After a few more exchanges Thrown and his gang retired into the complex at a run, guards giving them covering fire. Alarms began to sound throughout the compound.

"Not without what we came for!"

"I say we're dead either way," said Manuel, philosophically.

"And I need to visit with that one-armed robot," said I.

So it was hastily agreed. We had decided to go for it. Without the artifact we could never pay back the Makotai, who in several days would send every bounty hunter in the three systems after us. So we really didn't have much of a choice. Now was the time to make our raid and get the most valuable artifact in the known galaxy, now was the time to throw the dice.

"Charge, boodies!" Amoz cried.

Amoz led a charge across the square, his massive bulk

literally causing things to shake as he ran, firing at all points of incoming fire, chasing the remaining guards back into the buildings. With a yell, we followed. I stopped midway, at the bar, however, and grabbed a bottle of gin and took a giant swig.

"I needed that!" I said, and tucked the bottle into my belt.

As a rule I always fight a little better slightly buzzed. We halted at a the other side of the courtyard. The robot had fled east down a long tunnel, while Thrown and the guards headed west, up a long flight of stairs. I was always going after that robot.

"You guys go after Thrown and find the piece. I have a score to settle with that one-armed tin can."

Reinforcements had all ready arrived from the southern side of the courtyard. They started firing.

"I'll lure as many guards as I can my way."

"Molloy, you be careful."

"Why Lucy, you do care," I said. "I'll meet up with you guys as soon as I can. Now go!"

Lucy, Amoz and Manuel hurried up the stairs while I took another swig of gin. I turned and faced the oncoming guards and returned fire.

"What took you so long fellas?"

They responded typically, by shooting at me. I led them away, down that long hallway. Or to put it another way I heroically ran away as fast as I could. I usually run quite slow, but I am faster than a rabbit when motivated by a barrage of laser fire coming in my general direction. And these guys, unlike Memnon Vice, could actually aim. I was singed by two near misses, which prompted me to flee all the faster.

The hallway led into a wide room with machinery in it, some kind of heating/coolant chamber. There was no sign of the one-armed robot though, which was fine, as I needed to ditch the guards first before dealing with him, at any rate. There were half a dozen that had pursued me and I needed to quickly give them the slip.

I was wary, however, it being loud with various mechanical noises, and there were many things to hide behind in ambush.

Also, I had no idea where the one-armed robot might be. I took a moment to plot my next move and also, finally, removed my red and yellow target t-shirt. Aside from the obvious factor of wearing a target on your chest bright, primary colours clashed with my ego. Ducking out a side passage I almost walked right into another group of guards rushing towards me from a different direction. Firing blindly I ran through them, never sure if I hit any or not, but just running. There were yells and confusion. That was when the original pursuers collided with the newer group and it seems they must have blasted away at each other in the confusion. Not bothering to find out I ran on heroically, firing blindly behind me as I went. I ducked into another corridor and put as many twists and curves between myself and them as I could. I paused to catch my breath and took another pull of the gin and grimaced. My side was itching furiously. This was turning into one hell of a day.

I was perhaps doing too good a job at losing those pursuers though, and not a good enough one concerning the fate of my own quarry. I had no idea where that robot had got to. I wandered alone for several minutes and passed through several rooms. All were empty and all was quiet when suddenly a matte black arm was flung out from the shadows and I was knocked heavily into the wall. The one-armed robot loomed above me. I went to fire but his arm grabbed mine and would have crushed it had I not slammed the bottle of gin into his face, causing him to release me. He dripped of gin and his head was smoking slightly. One of his eyes went dead.

"Damn you shamus!"

On my back I crawled away from him, desperately trying to get some distance in between us. At close quarters I was no match for the robot's strength, even if he only had one arm, and we both new this.

"Molloy I am going to enjoy crushing the life from you!"

We both opened fire simultaneously, scrambling also to find cover. I hit him twice in the midsection, but the blasts deflected off, causing only minor damage. And I took a hit in the shoulder. It hurt, but wasn't too bad either. The robot and I were now on opposite sides of the room, he behind a large power container, which had heavy pipes and thick cables attached to it, snaking up the wall. I was behind a steal support pillar.

"Molloy, you shouldn't take these things so personally."

"I am getting very tired of people saying that," I replied.

We exchanged fire a couple times, but we were both protected by cover. And then I had an idea. I fired several shots at those heavy metal pipes and cables, mainly where they were bracketed to the wall and the whole section came down on top of him, along with half the wall. When the dust from all the debris cleared I made my way cautiously over to the pile. I needed to see, to make sure. I knew the robot would not give up until its mission was complete. He was pinned down. His legs were crushed and he was trying to pull himself free. He no longer had his hand-blaster. When he saw me he ceased his actions, and stared at me with that one working eye. All was eerily quiet except the occasional groan from the settling debris and rubble.

"Hey, robot, I never asked, what's your name?"

"R-7765-42."

The robot used all of its considerable strength to try and escape from the crush of heavy material pinning it, which seemed a hopeless task, especially with only one working appendage. The pile groaned, but didn't budge. I set my blaster on maximum force.

"Thanks. It was really getting awkward there for a while."

The robot winked at me and suddenly twisted brutally, breaking his torso free, leaving those mangled legs behind, still pinned beneath the debris. He dragged himself towards me, and then lunged, that one remaining limb swung out, poised to tear into me like a claw.

I blasted him three times dead centre, maximum power setting. And the one-armed-robot, a.k.a. R-7765-42, was forever no more.

<->

MEANWHILE the others were also having a tough go of it.

They had pursued Thrown and his people up those lengthy stairs, Manuel and Lucy quickly out-distancing Amoz, who was not built for speed. Inside a large chamber at the top they caught their breathe and awaited him. Like me they had quickly lost their prey. In this broad and richly decorated room there were several hallways leading off into different parts of the compound and one stairway leading up. There were no visible closets in site, to Manuel's great chagrin.

"Well Lucy, which way?"

"According to those schematics Lazslo showed us earlier Thrown's private quarters are that way," she said, pointing to a long corridor leading west."

"You'd think he'd be on the top floor."

"Yes, you would. And I don't fully trust that fellow."

Amoz arrived, slightly out of breath.

"Ahhh, hi there," said the big man. "So, the guards are coming."

Several laser blasts entered the room from the staircase as if to emphasize the point. In fact, not only were guards coming from the stairs below, but they also began pouring out of the hallways on either side of the chamber, in large numbers.

"I guess up the stairs it is," said Manuel.

He and Lucy started up the stairs, exchanging fire with the three fronts of guards now closing in, using the gilded banisters for what little cover they provided.

"Ugh, more stairs," grunted Amoz, and followed.

There occurred a slow running laser battle. Amoz, backing up the whole way, provided a lot of covering fire with his rifle, pinning the majority of guards down, allowing them time to escape to the next floor.

"There are no doors to bar or closets anywhere to be seen. This is really quite frustrating," said Manuel.

"Calm down Manuel. We need to lose these guards and find Thrown's living quarters. I'm sure he'd keep something that valuable close to him."

"The living quarters are that way," said Amoz over his shoulder, backing into the room, squeezing off an occasional blast whence he came.

He pointed down a hallway at the far end festooned with lush red carpet and velour.

"How do you know?" asked Manuel.

"It's the fanciest."

"He's right, of course. Cal-Ray Thrown made his fortune in red velour. We must be wary. But this will lead us to the inner sanctum. Come on boys!" said Lucy, who now rose proudly to her full height. "This will lead us to Thrown and the Famous Jewelled Phallus of Arkon III the Credulous, our prize and our salvation!"

Lucy lead the way into the aforementioned hallway with an overabundance of zeal, it might be said. The sounds of pursuit were all ready growing.

"Melodrama anyone?" said Manuel to no one in particular, following.

"Nice shag carpeting," added Amoz, once more taking up his position in the rear.

<->

MEANWHILE, I was leading yet more of those annoying guards on a merry chase, and with a near dead hand-blaster even. This last fact made it less than merry for me, but I am sure greatly increased the mood of my pursuers.

The problem with setting a blaster on its highest setting was that you then only had a limited amount of shots before the power supply goes dead, especially in a hand-blaster. Besides, a direct hit on a human with a blaster set on low, usually gets you a kill anyways, or at least takes them out of the fight. Those laser rifles Manuel and Amoz had pack a lot more juice, but I like a hand-blaster for concealment and wear-ability. And although the high setting had definitely been required in my personal and intimate duel with the one-armed robot my blaster was, as a result, running on fumes. To add to this irritation my shoulder was sore from where I took a hit and my shrapnel wound, perhaps jealous at the attention, had also started to act up.

And then there were those annoying guards that I couldn't seem to shake. I still had a few shots left and so fired back now and again, just to keep them from rushing me. Finally, after a few more twists and turns things quieted down some, meaning no one was in visible range and close enough to shoot at me. I always enjoyed not being shot at, but knew it wasn't likely to last. Especially as I could still hear sounds of their pursuit. However, after fifteen minutes of moving as quietly as I could from room to room, down narrow corridors, up stairs, I did shake even the sounds of pursuit and at last could catch my breath.

The place was built like a maze and I was more than slightly lost. But I also wasn't found, so that part kind of had worked out. All was a silence that was both eerie and welcomed. Investigating my surroundings it seemed I was in the service corridors for the place, the staff only areas of the complex. It certainly was poorly lit and dingy. I paused to look out a window and peered down onto the courtyard where we had almost met our grim fate if not for Amoz and his well timed rescue. Looking up at the tower where the prison cells were I noticed smoke billowing out some of the windows and wondered what might have occurred there.

"Interesting," I said, and made a mental note to try not talking to myself as much.

That's when I decided I needed to find me some information as being neither lost nor found no longer seemed to be a productive use of my time. And time was ticking. Some information, and a stiff drink, ideally. So when I heard someone coming I went towards the sounds and not away for the first time that day. A tall, thin, well coiffed man came around the bend. He was carrying a tray. I recognized that uniform, and it was no soldier's. This prompted me to step out of the shadows blocking his path, blaster levelled and pointing straight at the waiter's chest.

"Freeze. Now, don't move a muscle and you won't get hurt."

The waiter stopped, then raised his hands, which was not exactly obeying my command. I shrugged off this minor affront off, however.

"Are you what's causing all the alarm and commotion around here?"

"Yes. Me and my friends."

"Well, you know, some of us have jobs to do."

"You're a waiter."

"You figured that out all by yourself hotshot?"

"I was a waiter. So, you and I, we're comrades. I was one just last week. On a cruise ship."

"You don't look like a waiter, or smell like one."

"I've been moonlighting as a prisoner of late. We don't get showers. And also being about to be executed is rather a sweat inducing business."

"Being a waiter is definitely better than being executed."

"You're telling me."

"What ship were you on?"

"The Antipoinnes."

"Whew. Or maybe not," he said dryly. "I know that ship well."

"Look, I'm not going to hurt you. I just need some information."

"Most waiters don't carry hand-blasters either, far as I know."

"I know the waiter's code. I need your help."

"Pffft. The waiter's code states only be helpful if you expect a promising tip. Have a you a nice tip I should be expecting? Honey, I'll be upfront and just say it don't really look like it."

"I'm a little short seeing how I just escaped the firing squad. But I need to find Cal-Ray Thrown's living quarters."

"He's a bad tipper too."

"I could shoot you."

"That would break the waiter code. Rule 43: never shoot

a fellow waiter."

"Damn, you got me there."

"Listen, I'm running late, so I'll break my own rules and give you the tip, which is this: follow the red velour."

The waiter jerked his head behind, the way he had come.

"Now I really have to be going."

"How do I know you won't call the guards if I let you go."

"Same reason I know you won't shoot me in the back. The waiter's code."

"I admire your confidence."

And off he sauntered without bothering to respond. And since shooting an innocent waiter in the back wasn't really my style I let him go and hoped it wouldn't come back to haunt me. He seemed to have no love for Thrown though. I shrugged and headed the way he had indicated, looking for the red velour.

Of course, what I found was more guards, but luckily they hadn't found me. It appeared they were sentries and lost in conversation. So it appeared the waiter hadn't sold me out after all, or at least not as of yet. They were just two of them thankfully, guarding an entrance to a hallway, and not just any hallway, but a red velour one. There was to be no avoiding them so I cautiously and stealthily approached, keeping to the shadows and and out of their line of vision as much as possible.

"There's been a prisoner escape."

"Pffft, everyone knows that. Old news Dudo. From the execution."

"No, another one. From the cells, just a little while ago."

"Wow. That's a lot of escapes for a Tuesday."

"I know. Everyone is very upset."

"Be a guard, Mother said. It'll be easy. Just stand around and guard things, Mother said."

"I was voted most likely to guard things at school. That's so why I chose being a guard." "There's a nice pension, Mother said."

That's when I was close enough to hop out and unload on them. Luckily for them, they were only stunned. My hand-blaster was officially out of juice.

"Looks like it's your lucky day boys," I said, and proceeded to tie them up and disarm them. And then, one by one, I dragged them both into a shadowy corner.

"Lucky, lucky boys."

I took both of their blasters and headed down the distinctly velour hallway.

<->

SHAG carpeting and red velour; the quantities of it were staggering. There was red or pink velour on pretty much every surface. It was like a dream, or nightmare, depending on one's personal views of various fuzzy shades of red. As was for me, so too my boon companions. But unfortunately for the three of them they were in the process of walking directly into the jaws of a red and pink velour trap.

"Fighting to the death in this environment is absurd," Manuel scoffed, as they walked.

"I kind of like pink," said Amoz.

"Ick," said Lucy. "But at least this heavy shag muffles our footsteps some. And heads up guys, I feel we're getting close."

They entered a lavish chamber filled with couches and divans and diaphanous curtains. It was completely deserted. Above them and set at intervals all around the room were elegant balconies, also deserted.

"Now I know what paradise looks like," said Manuel.

"Paradise would never be so tacky," replied Lucy.

Directly across from them on the other side of the room was a slightly less grand, more private looking passageway. It was more subtly decorated, with pink flamingos.

"That must be it. The entrance to his inner-inner chambers," said Lucy.

"Where the closets will surely be," added Manuel.

"And our final goal," continued Amoz.

Suddenly guards rushed in from said doorway. The first three carried with them large deflector shields, which they propped up a few feet in front of the entrance, making a kind of fortified defensive position. Others followed them, weapons raised. These fell into position behind the shield-men, blasters lined up, resting on the shields.

"Space-balls!" cursed Manuel.

"We'll have to take out those guards," said Amoz.

"Yep," said Lucy. "Frekking huge space-balls."

"There's six and they have shielding," added Amoz.

"Fortune is said to favour the bold," said Manuel, with a wry smile. "Ready?"

The three rushed to the attack, weapons blazing. But until they reached closer quarters their laser blasts just deflected harmlessly off those deflector shields. They were now caught in open ground in the middle of the room. And that was when the trap was sprung. More guards arrived to seal off their rear. At the same time guards entered the room from both flanks, weapons charged and pointing. And above, in those beautiful balconies, guards appeared at intervals, armed with sniper blasters at the ready. There was a moment of silence, the calm before the storm. Amoz and Lucy and Manuel exchanged looks of trepidation steeled with determination. And then everyone opened up from everywhere.

"Amoz, make us some cover. Grab anything that's not nailed down," Lucy shouted. "Manuel, take out those balcony snipers forthwith!"

Weapon's fire was coming at them from all angles. Lucy was blasting away at foes on the ground level while Manuel, who was a crack shot, took out two of the balcony snipers high above. Amoz meanwhile lumbered forth and brought down a large marble column and piled three heavy couches around it to make a little make-shift bunker. However, and in the process, he was hit by two glancing laser blasts, which the giant shook off. The three of them then regrouped under the limited, but greatly improved cover Amoz had created. Lucy kept firing away, trying to keep those guards pinned down on the flanks. The cross-fire directed at them was murderous, however. She took out three of them on the right and one on the left, but there were many, many more. Manuel tagged another of the snipers, but also got hit in the leg with a fairly bad burn. Amoz, who had the hardest time finding cover, took another hit to his bulky frame. While Manuel and Lucy tried to regroup he laid down a steady fire in three directions.

"They must have been ordered to use low capacity firepower, afraid of burning the place down," shouted Lucy.

"It doesn't matter, at this rate we'll be cut to pieces before long," Manuel replied.

"I know," Lucy replied. "And the place will still burn down. We need to get through those shields."

They ducked low as sniper fire from above tore into the couch they sheltered behind, melting the material and frame, diminishing it considerably.

"Manuel, you need to take out those snipers!" shouted Lucy, before she was hit in the shoulder and fell back with a cry of pain.

They were pinned down and things were looking bleak. Lucy was wounded and momentarily out of the fight. But Manuel kept targeting those balcony snipers and took out one more, leaving only three of the best sheltered ones remaining. Meanwhile Amoz kept up a steady barrage, trying to pin the attackers down and keep them from returning fire. But the makeshift bunker he had created was doomed and inevitably on the verge of complete collapse. Several small fires were burning on it and throughout the room.

Suddenly there was a large explosion to the right, in the distance and out of sight. Immediately all those guards on the right flank moved to face this unknown new threat. Lucy had, meanwhile, recovered enough to rejoin the fight, her teeth clenched. She embraced Amoz and then Manuel. Smoke had begun to accumulate in the room, obscuring visibility.

"Now's our chance, under the cover of the smoke," shouted Manuel.

Amoz rose to his full, bulky height. He turned and looked at his two friends and smiled.

"Wait Amoz, no!" screamed Lucy.

Amoz hurled a unrecognizably burned couch headlong into the guards up front. It smashed into two of the shield-men, knocking them sprawling. He then charged them spraying their position with laser fire. He was immediately hit by cross fire, but carried on his charge with a roar. Manuel leapt from cover too, rolled, rose and fired three pin-point shots taking out all the remaining snipers with clean head shots. Lucy concentrated on those other guards to the left targeting Amoz as he ran the thirty feet remaining into the jaws of incoming laser fire. Again Amoz was hit, and with ten feet to spare, hit again. He went down to one knee and lost his rifle.

"Amoz, no!" shouted Lucy.

She tried to run to him, but was forced back by fierce enemy fire. More smoke was filling the room and fires were spreading at an alarming rate.

"They got Amoz, Manuel!"

Now, galvanized by rage and sadness, Manuel and Lucy started blasting away at anything moving, causing considerable damage and casualties. During this time Amoz struggled. He rose with difficulty, swaying a little. But then he steadied and charged one more time, crashing into the remaining guards blocking the way forward, sending them all sprawling, fleeing. And there he fell, but he had cleared the way. Manuel and Lucy ran after him shooting at anything and everything. They made it to the fallen giant and together hauled him to his feet and then all three slowly made it through into the narrow hallway beyond. They gently set him down in a pool of light coming from a large window, his body smoking and heavily burned. Lucy tended to him while Manuel contrived to block the entrance with a large desk, statue and cabinet he found in an adjoining chamber. Beyond, in the room they had escaped, there was sounds of general alarm as the fires spread and there were no immediate attempts at pursuit.

"I think the guards have their hands full with the fire and whatever caused that other explosion at the moment."

Lucy didn't answer Manuel. She was cradling Amoz's head in her lap. Manuel approached the two of them sadly.

"Amoz, you did real well. Amoz, you saved us," he whispered.

"Boodies," Amoz whispered weakly.

His eyes were shut. His body was covered in burns. His right arm hung limp at his side, at an unnatural angle.

"Amoz, you're going to be all right," said Lucy.

Amoz didn't answer. Lucy began to dig in the giant's pockets.

"Lucy, you shouldn't disturb him. He hasn't much time," said Manuel, sadly.

With a grunt Lucy pulled out another little remote control and pressed a series of buttons.

"I am calling the land-skiff. Manuel, get that window open."

Amoz stirred weakly and looked up a Lucy. His grimace turned into a smile. Manuel had to smash a glass pane, but got the window open.

"I helped, right... Lucy? You are my... friends... right? I always wanted... friends," Amoz gasped, on the verge of consciousness.

"Yes, Amoz. Friends. We, we love you," whispered Lucy is his ear, tears streaming down her face.

"We are the best of friends Amoz. Forever," said Manuel, staring sadly down at the broken giant.

"Good... Tell Molloy... goodbye. From his... friend... Amoz," he said, and then his eyes closed and he was still.

The land-skiff arrived and hovered just inside the window.

"You can tell him yourself when you're better," said Manuel, now also freely crying.

Together Manuel and Lucy pushed, shoved, dragged the prone body of Amoz, through the window and onto the skiff. They tied him onto it with some sash from the window's long curtains and then Lucy sent the skiff hurtling back towards the ship at top speed. Luckily the soldiers were still too busy to pursue them. The fire in that vast pleasure chamber was keeping them more than occupied. Manuel and Lucy hugged one another, both crying as they watched the skiff until finally it was lost from sight.

"Does the ship have a medical bay? I never asked it," said Manuel.

"It must. Of course, it must. I hope," said Lucy.

<->

THERE was a lot of smoke and commotion coming from an area I wisely decided to avoid. There had been several explosions also that I chose discretion over curiosity as regards to. Instead, I found a much quieter and less smoky path of the velour persuasion. This one had nice pink wall paper with flamingos on it. It would be absurd to die in a hallway with pink flamingo wallpaper, I rationalized, and so immediately began to feel considerably safer. However, my side ached and shoulder too. All and all I was becoming less and less enthused with the entire adventure. All I wanted to do was find Thrown, and/or Lucy, Amoz and Manuel, find the stupid artifact that was the only thing that could save our wretched lives, steal it, get back to Ship, and get the hell off this damned moon. And if I could find a nice stiff drink along the way, well that would be a nice bonus.

It was all very isolated and quiet. I figured I had made it through the security perimeter and was now somewhere in the inner sanctum. Sadly there wasn't a kitchen or bar in sight and this did nothing to improve my mood. As a result I had a blaster in each hand and was highly motivated to use them. After a few minutes searching through various rooms I came upon the first body. It was a guard, his throat slit ear to ear. Another fifty metres and I came upon another one. This one had been stabbed in the back and his neck was broken. Both guards had been disarmed. No wonder it was so quiet around here, I thought, everyone's dead. But something was bothering me. The brutality of the deaths for one thing, and also these guards had been killed with a knife or sharp edge and not blaster fire. It was peculiar and this lent to speculation that other parties might be involved. I decided to be extra cautious.

I paced through the eerily silent halls looking in this room and that. The place was deserted. That is until I rounded a corner and saw two more guards lying prone on the ground, and two shadowy figures looming over them. I cleared my throat, hand-blasters levelled and no messing about. It was an understatement to say I was relieved to discover it was Manuel, who wheeled and raised his rifle, and Lucy, who hissed like a cat.

"Didn't mean to sneak up on you."

"Molloy, you almost got yourself shot."

"I wasn't sure it was you. Did you kill all these guards? Seems a lot of over-kill, no pun intended."

"We didn't kill them. We found them this way, a minute ago," said Manuel. "Molloy, it's good to see you still alive and in one piece."

"It's good to be still alive. And likewise."

Lucy turned back to continue her examination of the dead men. I noted that these had been killed by blaster fire, not knife wounds like the others I had found.

"These men were murdered with skill, the precision of an assassin," said Lucy.

"Well, there's two more back that way I came, except they were stabbed. If it wasn't you guys I reckon we might now have some competition."

"Someone else is after Thrown and the artifact."

"It's a good bet. And whoever it is is a real pro. I've been following a trail of corpses like breadcrumbs."

Manuel stood up and we embraced. It was good to see them both alive and in one piece too. I nodded to Lucy and squeezed her on the shoulder.

"Where's Amoz?"

Both of their faces fell and I immediately braced myself for the worst.

"Amoz fell, in battle. He saved us, but he..."

"He got shot up pretty bad. Without him we'd be dead for sure."

"Where is he?"

"He was hurt real bad, and not conscious. We got the skiff and sent him back to the ship."

"Will he make it?"

"Molloy, it looks grim. He took a lot of hits."

"We said our goodbyes. He wanted us to tell you goodbye."

"I figured at the least we can give him a proper burial at space, if we survive all this," said Manuel.

"That's a big if," I said.

Lucy rose to her feet and stared at each of us hard in the eyes.

"We need to finish this now. Once and for all," said Lucy.

She was right. I was beginning to learn she was usually right, and harder than Manuel and I combined.

"For Amoz," said Lucy.

"For Amoz!" we replied.

The two dead guards had been guarding a door, which was left slightly ajar, likely by whomever had killed them. We moved cautiously through it and into the room beyond. My trigger fingers were itching. I wanted revenge, for Amoz. I wanted a fight, but what we found instead, sprawled about across the room, were another four dead guards. Each had been killed by a single laser blast to the head. There was another door at the other side of the room. It was heavily decorated with gold and red, carved intricately with flamingos.

"He also loved flamingos," whispered Lucy. "This is it. Come on."

But she suddenly motioned for silence. There was a commotion on the other side of that door. We listened to a muffled argument.

"Guards! Guards!! help me!"

"I think you'll find your personal guards won't answer. They won't answer to anybody, ever again."

"I should have executed you personally, when I had the chance."

"You underestimated me Thrown. Now hand it over. Ten years I've been waiting for this moment."

We entered the room as quietly as we could. The drama

was taking place around a corner. It seemed to be between Thrown and another man. We approached quietly, weapons at the ready.

"You won't get away with this! Guards! What is it, lunch time? Guards!"

"I think the majority are rather occupied chasing that fool Molloy or trying to put out the fires I set."

"The fire suppression will have been activated and they will be here any moment and when they arrive..."

"When they arrive you'll be dead, and I'll be gone, with the prize."

I peeked around the corner and there saw two men. Thrown, and facing him, blaster pointed at his chest was none other than Lazslo Loewenstein. The place had all ready been trashed and Thrown was clutching something wrapped in cloth defiantly to his chest.

"Now, I will not ask you again, give me the artifact! Give me the Famous Jewelled Phallus of Arkon III the Credulous!"

That was our cue. We sprang around the corner weapons readied, but Lazslo was fast. He spun cat-like, immediately turned his blaster on us. As he did this Thrown took the opportunity to pull a concealed hand-blaster of his own. It was a three way Plutonian standoff. We all eyed one another nervously. Thrown's blaster was visibly trembling, but his eyes were cold and deadly. Lazslo, though swollen and bruised, looked calm, business-like.

"All right everyone, don't move. Lazslo, hand over the blaster. Thrown, you too," said I.

"Not going to happen."

"Not a chance. The guards will be coming any moment," said Thrown. "Nice to see you Lucy. However, you look a lot less deader than I'd hoped."

"We're here for the artifact Thrown. Give it up and you might live to buy some more flamingos."

"Leave now Lucy, and I might not have you properly executed this time."

"I see we're at a bit of an impasse," I said. "Lazlso, I am

impressed. You are one tough cookie."

"Everyone always underestimates Lazslo. Now all of you, put down the blasters and I'll let you walk away alive. No one has to die if I get what I want."

Lazslo was cool, cold, calculating. And several other words starting with the letter 'c'. He was determined and, judging by what he had done to all those guards, ruthless. He was clearly not to be trifled with. But then, none of us were.

"We can't do that Lazslo. Without that artifact we all get death warrants, courtesy of the Makotai."

"Making deals with the Makotai Molloy? Not your wisest move."

"It wasn't my idea Lazslo. The problem with having associates. Say speaking of, what about that missing daughter of yours?"

"There never was a daughter. Not on this forlorn moon anyways."

I chewed on that for a while. Lazslo played us, used us, but then we were using him too, and had been all along. And slippery as the bastard was, he did save us from the Memnon P.D. I kept my hand-blasters firmly centred on him as he seemed the most potent threat. No one was backing down and things were poised on a knife edge. One split second twitch, miscue or misfire could set everyone off.

"If anyone shoots, we'll probably all end up dead," said Thrown, breaking the silence. "And my guards will be coming any moment. I suggest you all leave at your quickest convenience."

"Your guards killed our friend Amoz, you shotak jeek!"

"What did you expect? You broke into my house, caused untold damage, ruined my morning execution. Not to mention, do you have any idea how much those guards cost?"

"Everyone needs to calm down."

"Lazslo's the one who killed most of the guards," said Manuel, petulantly.

If things were out of hand before they were rapidly getting worse. Thrown was looking increasingly agitated.

"And you, Lucy, broke my heart."

"Thrown, you knew what we had was what it was."

"If everyone is to die, then so be it! I will take you all with me! This pistol is set to atomize!"

"Everyone has the drop on everyone. No one can win," I said, trying to calm things down.

"I'll take my chances with you amateurs," said Lazslo.

"Who's he calling amateurs? You were a drunk at a bar when we met you!" stuttered Manuel.

All I could think of was getting the prize and escaping, and then mourning poor Amoz and getting off this godforsaken rock. We all eyed one another. I had my blasters aimed at Lazslo and he at me, while Lucy and Manuel targeted Thrown who's own blaster kept wavering from target to target to target.

"Don't shoot the artifact whatever you do," said Lucy.

And then Manuel sneezed.

Everyone started shooting and diving for cover simultaneously. While Lazslo was firing wildly at me he was charging Thrown, diving for the artifact, and that is maybe why he missed. In fact, none of us hit our targets, such was the chaos and panic in the room. Lazslo was on Thrown in an instant, had knocked his weapon away and the two grappled, locked in a life or death struggle for the object Thrown clung to so desperately. And then Lucy joined the fray, fighting just as, if not more, viciously. They clawed and beat at one another, rolling along the floor, shouting and cursing, pulling and twisting. Someone's hand tore at the fabric of the artifact and a black, shadowy phallic shape emerged.

"Manuel, don't look at it. The curse!" I said, partially covering my eyes, waiting for Lucy to move so I could get in a clean shot.

Lucy took a kick to the stomach and was knocked free of the struggling mass. Myself and Manuel looked at one another and levelled our weapons. It was time to end this. At our backs in the distance we could hear the commotion of approaching guards. They would be upon on us in moments.

Lazslo and Thrown, intent on one another, had no idea the

jeopardy they were in. Each stubbornly clung to the artifact, trying to wrest it free of the other. Manuel and I were about to open up on both of them when suddenly it slipped from both man's grasp. It flew up in the air and seemed almost to hang there. Everyone froze. All eyes must have been drawn to it, despite the curse. Mine certainly were. This was the item so many had fought and died for. It was plain and black, and phallic shaped. What puzzled me was that it was not very jewel encrusted at all. It hung in the air for a second as if the gravity had been turned off. And then it fell to the ground and smashed into a hundred pieces.

"Wait, it can't break! No, this is impossible!" said Lazslo.

"It is made of unbreakable adamantine," said Thrown. "Unless..."

"This is not possible," said Lazslo, on his knees.

Thrown started laughing, giggling uncontrollably. "A fake. The whole time, it's been a fake."

The guards were coming. I helped Lucy, who was still winded and breathing in quick gasps, to her feet. She turned her hand-blaster on Thrown who was now bent over, doubled over with laughter.

"I was so afraid of the curse..." he said, barely able to speak through his laughter.

Lazslo was on his knees holding pieces of the artifact, which crumbled in his hands like sand.

"No, no! Ten years I have been searching for this. It can't be fake."

Lucy lowered her blaster. She then took out the remote and called for the skiff.

As guards came rushing in Manuel and I turned our attention to them and we had a bit of a secondary standoff until the skiff arrived. No one shot anyone though. Thrown was laughing through much of it, tears streaming down his face. Lazslo sat sprawled on the ground, his face painted in disbelief. The skiff arrived and we boarded it from the room's balcony. The guards did not attempt to stop us. Thrown gave no orders to. He seemed content to let us leave. He was still chuckling.

He almost seemed to be darkly enjoying the absurdity of it all. No one else wanted to die, or needed to, as it turned out. The entire thing we had fought for, fought over, was nothing but a fake, a fraud, a joke.

The last thing I heard before we left was Thrown talking to Lazslo.

"Well Lazslo, shall we partner up. Begin the search again?"

# THE END

# EPILOGUE

# EPILOGUE

B ACK ON THE SHIP. Our ship. Which was now officially named Ship.

We were off-moon and heading into deep space. Head away from trouble, is the exact instructions Lucy had told Ship. And so it had. We were exhausted, broke, hungry and likely all ready had our death warrants issued to every bounty hunter in the three systems. But nonetheless, things were looking up.

The three of us crowded around two medical beds pushed together that housed the giant frame of a very weak and beaten up, but alive and on the mend, Amoz. That was the reason things were looking up. The ship indeed had possessed a medical bay, and a top notch one at that. Amoz was happily sipping from a straw some terrible looking concoction of pain killers and nutrients designed to help him heal. His broken arm was properly set in a poly-fibre cast and his laser burned body was covered with healing salve gel-pads. He may have looked like a complete mess but, according to Ship, he was healing nicely and would make a full recovery. He was smiling, half awake. We were all smiling.

"Boodies," he said, before drifting back into unconsciousness.

We each in turn approached and gently touched our gentle giant. It was a touching, emotional moment. We had all grown very fond of Amoz.

Suddenly the ship shuddered violently.

"Ah, I hate to interrupt the love-in guys," said Ship, "but you three are needed on the bridge. We are currently under attack."

We immediately rushed towards the bridge as the ship was wracked by several more shuddering convulsions. From the sounds and intensity it appeared our shields were holding. For the time being. We rushed onto the bridge and strapped ourselves into our respective seats.

"Ship, status report," said Lucy.

"One ship has engaged us. I am attempting countermeasures, evasive manoeuvres. Weapons standing by."

"Bounty hunters!" said Manuel.

"I don't want a fight. Ship, can you disable their engines? Outrun them?" asked Lucy.

"Preliminary scans suggest yes. One precise laser attack should disable their engines."

"Do it Ship. Damage report?"

"Minimal damages to report," said Ship. "Shields holding. Laser barrage successful."

"Good. Get us out of here."

Ship put some distance between us and our pursuers. We headed into open space and left the first of many, many bounty hunters in our wake.

I had been keeping a low profile. I figured Lucy was much more captain material than I. I put my feet up and looked out the rear-view-screen and let out a sigh of relief as the formerly attacking vessel was reduced to tiny speck, and then lost among the stars.

"Hey Manuel, what does semantics mean?"

MILITARY GRADE

**MUTANT**
SPIDER-CIDE

70CL 140% VOL.

53394855R00102

Made in the USA
San Bernardino, CA
16 September 2019